A RUSSIAN

THREE NOVELLAS

Cherry
Orchard
Books

A RUSSIAN IMMIGRANT

THREE NOVELLAS

MAXIM D. SHRAYER

BOSTON

2019

Library of Congress Cataloging-in-Publication Data

Names: Shrayer, Maxim, 1967—author. | Container of (work): Shrayer, Maxim,
  1967—Bohemian spring. | Container of (work): Shrayer, Maxim, 1967—
  Brotherly love. | Container of (work): Shrayer, Maxim, 1967—Borscht belt.
Title: A Russian immigrant: three novellas / by Maxim D. Shrayer.
Description: Boston: Cherry Orchard Books, an imprint of Academic Studies
  Press, 2019.
Identifiers: LCCN 2019007682 (print) | LCCN 2019016837 (ebook) |
ISBN 9781644690376 | ISBN 9781644690369 (pbk.)
Subjects: LCSH: Immigrants—United States—Fiction. | Jews, Russian—United States—
Fiction.
Classification: LCC PG3487.R34 (ebook) | LCC PG3487.R34 A6 2019 (print) |
DDC 891.73/44—dc23
LC record available at https://lccn.loc.gov/2019007682

Cover design by Ivan Grave based on a photo by Maxim D. Shrayer.

Illustrations in the text are based on photos by the author.

Photos © 2019 by Maxim D. Shrayer.

Published by Cherry Orchard Books, an imprint of Academic Studies Press, in 2019.

Academic Studies Press
1577 Beacon Street
Brookline, MA 02446
P: (617) 782-6290
F: (857) 241-3149
press@academicstudiespress.com
www.academicstudiespress.com

To the Russian workingmen whose unstinted toil helps to maintain the basic industrial mechanism of America, but who for the most part are by this very service kept out of reach of the warm, friendly heart of our people.

—Jerome Davis, *Russian Immigrant* (1922)

"Avtomobil', kostyum—nu pryamo amerikanets (a veritable American), pryamo Ayzenhauer!" said Varvara, and introduced Pnin to Roza Abramovna Shpolyanski.

—Vladimir Nabokov, *Pnin* (1957)

Raskolnikov, the student, gave him a pain, with all his miseries. Frank first had the idea he must be a Jew and was surprised when he found out he wasn't.

—Bernard Malamud, *The Assistant* (1957)

Contents

BOHEMIAN SPRING

Six years passed since Simon Reznikov and his parents had come to America as refugees, and they were now eligible for naturalization. In January 1993 Simon, Yakov and Inga Reznikov, formerly of Moscow, were sworn in as new US citizens at a Boston courthouse. Simon was twenty-six, a doctoral student. His field was comparative literature, and émigré women his mother's age told him he looked a bit like a young Pasternak, except he didn't limp and had bright blue eyes and reddish curly hair.

Simon drove up to Boston from New Haven for the naturalization ceremony. In the evening there was a celebration at a Russian restaurant in Brookline, to which his parents invited local family and friends, some of them—also old refuseniks and new Americans, others—the lucky ones who had gotten out before the sluices of Jewish emigration were closed in 1980. His parents' Russian friends and relatives—even those who still thought of themselves as "the intelligentsia"—had trouble with Simon's choice of career. Only his Moscow childhood friend Styopa Agarun, who had known him since the age of zero, got it, or at least did a good job pretending that he understood why Simon wanted to become a professor of literature. A literary professional rather than a doctor, a lawyer, or a programmer—that Jewish-Russian troika of American trades...

At the party Simon sat next to his cousin Yuri, a realtor, who had majored in history at Brandeis but chose real over unreal estate. Yuri was already married and living in a condo near Coolidge Corner. Simon's cousin was only two years older, but with him Simon felt like a raw youth.

"I know, Yurasha, I know. I could write my poems and sell condos to Russian booklovers," Simon whispered to his cousin as they kissed and hugged near the cloakroom.

"Syomka, I'll show you ropes," Yuri replied in English, juggling and dropping the definite article. "It's not too late."

In Russian they called him "Syoma" or "Syomka," sometimes "Syomochka." Diminutives didn't mean the same thing in America.

Three months later, research brought Simon to Prague, where the archive of Felix Gregor had turned up in a vault of the Czech National Library. Gregor had spent most of his short life in Prague. Born in 1900, he studied philosophy at the University of Vienna. He returned to Prague in 1922 and managed his father's pharmacy while writing novellas in German and poems in Czech. He died just seven months before the Munich Agreement, age thirty-eight, of what was probably lung cancer. Gregor was rediscovered after the war, and his name became well known in the West. He was, however, a writer without a biography. With the exception of a short memoir by Axel Freynt, a high school friend of Gregor's, who had escaped before the war, ended up in Montreal and become his literary executor, not too much was known about Gregor's private life. Many of his family and friends were murdered during the war, and his letters disappeared with them. And there was also Gregor's correspondence with his close friend, Countess Klara Rittenberg, which her Swiss heirs had published, in expurgated form, in the 1970s.

When Simon heard from his dissertation adviser, Professor Aurach, about Gregor's papers in Prague, he didn't think twice. Aurach, who as a teenager had left Czechoslovakia on a *Kindertransport*, had many connections in the expatriate community. Simon faxed a letter to the Czech National Library, Professor Aurach's endorsement appended to it. The reply came from the director of the Library, who promised "every form of assistance with your significant research." Speedily Simon applied for summer funding, booked a ticket, and started making arrangements to travel to the Czech Republic in the spring of 1993.

With the assistance of Aurach, Simon got hold of a mysterious man by the name of Vítek Chmela, a translator from English and a former Czech dissident who now ran a foreign-language bookshop in Prague and rented rooms to visiting Americans and Canadians. Simon telephoned Prague and spoke with Chmela's wife, Irenka. He was hesitant to use Russian and they ended up communicating in German. Irenka told Simon the room was ten dollars a day; he chuckled and rented it for five weeks.

Three weeks later he was on the plane from New York to Prague, perusing a pocket grammar of Czech. In Simon's carry-on there were three volumes of Gregor's fiction in English translation, xeroxed pages of his fiction in German and his Czech poetry, and many rolls of black and white film alongside a manual Pentax. Simon was sipping Becherovka—served on Czech Air in lieu of both aperitif and digestive—sipping the honeyed liqueur and mapping out a plan for the next six weeks.

Three years had passed since the Velvet Revolution and only three months since the Velvet Divorce. Americans were only beginning to discover Prague. Simon landed in Prague in early April on a cloudy afternoon. It was a small, Soviet prison-style terminal, with military vehicles parked on either side of the runway. Being an American citizen meant that he didn't need a visa, and twenty minutes after landing Simon was already riding to Prague in an orange Opel taxicab. He pretended not to speak any Slavic languages and gave the cabby a piece of paper with the address.

"I know that street," the cabby said in German. "Behind the Strahov Monastery. Nice area, private homes. Germans are now buying villas there. As an investment."

"How about Americans?" Simon asked.

"Nah, the Americans are mostly young people. Tend to live in the old center. Nice kids, naive."

They were entering Prague from the west side. The two-lane highway with binary potholes eventually became a city street with tram tracks down the middle. These two-humped, Czech-made red and white trams once populated the streets of Simon's Moscow childhood. He looked out at the people and the store signs. Old ladies in wool coats and kerchiefs carried groceries in mesh bags.

"Here it is, Bělohorská Street," said the cabbie. "We turn right here, and Tejnka is a few blocks up."

They turned into a narrow street and stopped in front of a wooden gate. As the cabby was hauling Simon's big suitcase of yellow leather, a tall, forty-something woman wearing a short skirt and a sleeveless blouse came out of the house.

"I'm Irenka, Pan Chmela's wife," she said loudly in Czech and waved to Simon. "Welcome to Prague." She was the epitome of a West Slavic woman, Simon thought to himself.

The house had a tile roof the color of old cork. Simon noticed a well and a vegetable patch in the back of the garden.

Irenka had watery blue eyes, a chiseled nose, long blonde hair, a large mouth with moist lips. Her motions were round and slow. She took Simon to his room.

"This is like a private apartment," she explained in German. "You have your own bedroom and an en suite."

"When do you want me to pay?" Simon asked in his stilted German.

"You'll pay my husband," Irenka answered. "The room comes with breakfast, and I'll serve it the garden." She paused, giggling. "Unless it's raining. Then I'll bring it to you."

Simon's bedroom had two narrow cots and a heavyset armoire. A ceramic dish with three oranges and a bottle of mineral water had been placed on a side table.

When Simon, showered and changed, came out to the garden, Irenka brought out a bowl of mushroom barley soup. While he ate, she asked how his family ended up in America.

"Do you miss home?" Irenka asked him.

"New Haven?"

"No, Moscow."

"Moscow isn't home anymore," Simon answered, a bit gruffly, and changed the subject to politics and the recent dissolution of Czechoslovakia.

Before sending Simon off to the center of Prague, Irenka circled the location of her husband's bookshop on the map and pointed him in the direction of the nearest tram stop.

At the bottom of the hill Simon boarded a tram. He rode it to Malostranské Square, where he got off and walked towards the Charles Bridge. Vítek's bookshop was off Staroměstské Square—the heart of old Prague. With the Soviet penchant for simple social classification still unflushed from his veins, Simon quickly identified three categories of Prague denizens. The first were the retirees; anxious-looking, dressed in Soviet-style, modest garb. The second were the young people. Scanning the crowd, Simon had the feeling that Prague had just woken up after a long winter of hibernation. Miniskirts were everywhere, and black lycra shorts—the kind people in America would wear to the gym and to ride bicycles—were the rage. Young women wore lycra shorts with a nice blouse, a T-shirt, or a sweater. Young men sported denim jackets; many greased their hair. Finally, Simon noticed a group of well-dressed men and women in their late thirties and early forties. Those, he presumed, were the Prague nouveaux riches. They walked slowly—the women on the arms of their male companions—carrying themselves with punctuated pride. The "new Czech" men favored purple double-breasted jackets and particolored ties. Their women had stiletto heels and fishnet stockings.

Vítek Chmela was a shortish bespectacled man with a clipped mustache and tobacco-stained teeth. He was dressed in faded jeans, suede shoes, and a wool cardigan over a grey turtleneck. It was about six in the evening, and Vítek still had several customers looking at old books. He asked Simon to wait for him at a beer cellar next door.

"Order yourself something to eat. Later we'll have a beer together and talk." Vítek spoke accurate English with a strong accent.

Surly waiters in soiled white shirts and black vests darted back and forth. The menu consisted of bread dumplings and pork dishes with various incarnations of potatoes. Simon, who avoided pork, asked for dumplings with gravy and a side of boiled potatoes. By the time Vítek joined Simon in the cellar, he had already had two pints of pilsner and was attempting to communicate in Czech with people at the next table. Vítek ordered a round of beer, and an hour later Simon had left Moscow and landed in Vienna, where Soviet refugees tasted freedom, and where Vítek had almost escaped in 1969—except he didn't get to the border before it was sealed.

On the way back they stopped at what Vítek called his "neighborhood pub." The owner greeted Vítek as an old friend.

"Workers from my district come here after the day shift and stay for the rest of the evening," Vítek explained. "And the ones who work the night shift come here in the morning and sometimes stay until closing."

When they finally left the pub, swearing eternal love for Dostoevsky, they had to hold on to each other during the ascent to Vítek's house on the hill.

"Welcome to Prague." Vítek pressed his hand into Simon's. "I hope you sleep well."

Simon woke up to the sounds of Irenka's chirpy *"Das Frühstück ist fertig."* It was after nine o'clock. He found a tray with breakfast on the wooden table: a plate with sliced cold chicken and cheese, two soft-boiled eggs, a sliced cucumber, a basket with bread rolls, ramekins with butter, sautéed mushrooms, homemade preserves, and a pot of black tea. Apple trees were in full bloom, and their dainty petals were everywhere—on the wooden table and benches, the ground, even the back of the Chmelas' orange cat.

On his first morning in Prague Simon put on a white shirt, chinos, and a blue blazer to look a hundred-proof American. As he walked down the hill to the tram stop, he observed the morning motions of this old Prague neighborhood: apartment windows were opened and pyramidal pillows placed on the windowsill to be aired and dried. Simon caught a tram to Malostranské Square, crossed the Charles Bridge, and headed for the Klementinum, formerly a monastery, later a Jesuit college, and now a complex of libraries.

The director of the Czech National Library, Renata Seifertová, with whom Simon had communicated by fax, was a Gertrude Stein look-alike with short white hair, a gray woolen dress, and a landscape agate brooch on her chest. She spoke in a husky voice and chain-smoked. Her Russian was very fluent and only slightly accented. In her office, Dr. Seifertová sat Simon down on a leather divan and served him a cup of strong instant coffee. Then she got straight to the point.

"Mr. Reznikov, your dissertation will be an important book."

"Dr. Seifertová, I'm flattered, but what makes you think so?" Simon asked. "Have you seen my articles about Felix Gregor?"

"No, my English isn't very strong. German and French are a different story. Russian, of course. But I've spoken about you with a couple of émigré friends of mine who teach at North American universities."

She mentioned the names of a Czech literature professor at Columbia and a historian at McGill.

"They speak highly of you. And, of course, we all admire your adviser, Professor Aurach. So let me be blunt. I'm an old woman, and I've lived through Nazism and Communism. Gregor's papers are among our prized possessions. Our archivists are nearly finished cataloguing them, and—along with Professor Archibald Cronin of Queensland University who left here last week—you are the only other Westerner to work with Gregor's archive."

"Thank you, Dr. Seifertová. I'm really honored."

"Call me *Paní Renato*! Here at the library we have quite an informal atmosphere. Some of us have been working together for thirty-five, even forty years."

"Thank you, *Paní Renato*."

"We see you as our guest from the future." The director launched a tirade. "As a former Soviet—and an American—you are familiar with life both in Eastern Europe and in the West. You are young and ambitious. We want you to accomplish as much of your research here as you can, then go back to America, and be our messenger there. We've got a lot of precious materials here, but our own funding is meager." The director picked up a heavy black receiver and made a phone call. "Tamara Zrzavá is our expert archivist," she said to Simon. "She'll be helping you with Gregor's papers."

Two minutes later there was a scratch at the director's leather-upholstered door. Paní Zrzavá, a woman of about fifty-five, small, skinny and flat-chested, entered the director's office. Her thin, yellowish hair was arranged in two braids held together by black rubber bands. Over her dress she wore a black satin robe of the sort that cleaning ladies used to don in the Soviet Union. Clutched in her fist she held a pair of spectacles; another pair—the plastic kind—too big for her small sallow face, was enthroned on the bridge of her bony nose. As she pulled her lips apart in a semblance of a smile, Simon saw horsey brown teeth.

"Paní Zrzavá," the director said in Russian. "This is Simon Reznikov, our scholar from America. I leave him in your able hands."

Dr. Seifertová got up, shook Simon's hand, and gently nudged him and the lady archivist to the door.

"Your name sounds so American. Did Simon use to be 'Semyon?'" Paní Zrzavá asked in Russian.

"Yes … Americanized along the way," Simon answered.

"I thought so," Paní Zrzavá said, pursing her lips.

Thinking of Ariadne and the Minotaur, Simon followed her down a labyrinth of stacks.

"Your parents are from Russia?" he asked after they reached Paní Zrzavá's nook.

"My mother is. My father was a Czech Jew. But I consider myself Russian." Paní Zrzavá spoke an émigrée's prewar Russian, unblemished and frozen in time.

Over tea with lemon and sugar cubes, Simon learned that her mother had grown up in St. Petersburg, and her father had come from outside Brno but went to medical school in Prague, where her parents met at a charity auction in the late 1920s. After the deportations began in 1941, a former patient hid her father, an obstetrician, in the Moravian countryside until the end of the war.

"There are still some of us left here in Prague, children of Russian émigré parents," said Paní Zrzavá. Then she glanced at her watch and sighed. "It's past one o'clock, and I promised Dr. Seifertová to give you an overview of Gregor's papers."

Simon detected anxiety in her voice and said: "I should, perhaps, explain a bit more what I'm looking for." Paní Zrzavá folded her hands on her lap and looked at him somberly through her thick lenses. "I'm interested in Gregor's last years. I want to know what he read, what he was thinking about, whom he socialized with. And three specific things. One is his Jewishness in the climate of the middle 1930s, the growing threat of Nazism—why am I even telling you this? The second is his relationship with Klara Rittenberg."

"Yes, her," Paní Zrzavá said, frowning. "And the third?" she asked.

"The third is . . . well . . . any unpublished or unfinished works by Gregor. I know he wrote very little after 1937 and his breakup with Klara. But he must have written something. Notes. Drafts. Anything."

"Klara Rittenberg, Gregor's femme fatale." A hemlocky smile flashed across Paní Zrzavá's face. "Everyone wants to know about her. I think she ruined his life."

"But she inspired him, didn't she?" Simon asked.

"Let me show you the archive," Paní Zrzavá replied, changing the subject. "As you know, Gregor never kept a diary. He believed one could never be honest with oneself on a page of a journal or diary."

She took Simon to a little reading room with two rectangular oak tables. A stained glass window let through feeble sunrays. Two green lamps atop the table were the main source of light.

"Please wait here. I'll bring Box One. There are three altogether. The third contains Gregor's books, and also periodicals and collections with his publications. There are corrections in the margins. Professor Cronin, when he was here, spent a lot of time on Box Three."

When Paní Zrzavá returned with a cardboard box, her instructions to Simon were: "When you are finished going through the contents, find me in the stacks. And please use these," she said and handed him a pair of white cotton gloves.

Simon was shaking when he opened the box and touched its rustling contents with the fingertips of both hands. He pulled out one folder after another, leafing through pages of Gregor's manuscripts and typescripts . . .

Felix Gregor wasn't prolific. His entire German oeuvre consisted of a novel, published in Frankfurt in 1927, three novellas, about two dozen short stories, and a handful of occasional essays and reviews. Add to this three slim volumes of his Czech-language poetry, and that's all Gregor was believed to have written. Simon made a checklist of the manuscripts: the first draft and the corrected typescript of the novel; manuscripts of the novellas and about half of Gregor's stories; poems scribbled down on the backs of prescription forms.

Simon took a lunch break and wandered about Staroměstské Square, looking for something other than a Czech pub. He finally found a little bistro and ordered a salad. He sat at the bar and chewed on lettuce and cucumbers, unable to shake the archive frenzy. It's like a drug, he was thinking. You cannot stop; you want more manuscripts; you crave the nirvana of discovery yet prolong its postponement. The bartender had long pine-dust hair and a deeply cut yellow shirt. She was wiping glasses and plates, taking her time, swaying to jazzy tunes. Her name was Jarka, she told Simon, and she was studying clinical psychology.

Simon returned to the library and examined the contents of Box One again, to make sure he hadn't missed anything. No, these were all manuscripts of previously published works, and they weren't going to do much for him. He went to find Paní Zrzavá at her desk, but she was gone. A pair of her wire-rimmed glasses was spread out on her desk, like a dead lark. A black-and-white photo, scratched and yellowed, showed a portly smiling man with a bowtie and a gentle young woman in a white dress against the background of a lake.

"You must be the researcher from America?" a female voice asked in English.

Simon turned around and saw a young woman with piercingly intelligent eyes, downcast as though they were distrustful of their own intelligence.

"That would be me."

"I'm Milena Krupičková. I work as an assistant here in the archives."

"It's very nice to meet you, Milena," Simon said to the young Czech woman with long legs and beautiful hands.

"Yes, thanks," Milena blushed. "Paní Zrzavá had to leave because of her mother. . . . Heart trouble again."

Simon looked again at Paní Zrzavá's desk.

"Paní Zrzavá said you would be welcome to look at more materials tomorrow," said Milena, picking up the box. "We close in half an hour."

Milena's eyes were green, her hair chestnut with a golden sheen. She wore a denim skirt and a cream button-up shirt.

"Milena, what do you say we have a glass of wine together—to celebrate my first day of work with Gregor's papers?" Simon asked.

"You wish to go together?" asked Milena. She spoke English well, but had some difficulty understanding Simon's American accent.

"Yes, I wish to go together," Simon said, imitating her intonation. And they both started laughing.

He waited for Milena outside, in the library's tenebrous courtyard. She came running down the chipped granite steps, swinging a red satchel in her right hand.

"I know a wine bar nearby," Milena said. "It is a 'very cool place,' as you say in America."

The bar was around the corner from Vítek Chmela's bookshop.

"I like this bookshop very much," Milena said. "Mr. Chmela is well known here. He was a dissident and very brave and principled. His first wife denounced him."

"Now he has another wife," Simon said. "She's younger. And makes a serious breakfast."

They took their glasses outside the bar and sat on the sidewalk, leaning against the wall. They sipped red wine and talked for a long time—first about Gregor, then about life under Communism and the Velvet Revolution, which occurred when Milena was a junior at Charles University. And about the recent dissolution of Czechoslovakia.

"We, Czechs, are a peaceful nation," Milena said. "The Slovaks are different. They are militaristic. Have you heard their anthem?"

Simon didn't know the Slovak anthem. "Let me get us some more wine," he offered.

"It's a little cold here," Milena said.

They settled inside the bar at a small table with a view of the spindly, cobble-stoned street.

"What do you make of the story of Felix Gregor and Klara Rittenberg?" Simon asked.

"It's very romantic, very Czech," Milena replied.

"Why do you think she went to Switzerland?"

"She sensed where things were going with the German expansion. She was a leftist, you know, left of our ruling Socialists. Very unusual for her time."

"So she went to Switzerland and left Gregor behind?" Simon asked.

"They never stopped loving each other," Milena said. "But he was Jewish, and she was an aristocrat."

"I'm also Jewish," Simon said.

"I know you are," Milena replied.

"And you are also a Czech aristocrat?" Simon joked.

"Far from it. My father sells fertilizers. He comes from generations of farmers. He only moved to Prague in the 1970s to attend a technical university."

"Where did he move from?" Simon asked.

"Oh, a small Moravian town near Brno," Milena answered. "I still have family there."

"And your mother?"

"She's from Prague, a regular Czech family. You would call it 'middle class.'"

Simon touched Milena's left hand with the index and middle fingers of his right hand. "I'll still think of you as my Czech aristocrat."

"And I'll think of you as my American," Milena said seriously, without removing his hand.

"Russian-American," Simon corrected her. "But how did you know I was Jewish?"

"I just know . . ." Milena suddenly grew quiet, straightening her hair. "We should probably go."

It became dusky outside. A cold wind blew from the Vltava as they walked towards the Charles Bridge.

Milena and Simon said goodbye at the tram circle, and he scribbled down Vítek Chmela's phone number on a used ticket. Her tram came first, a clanking creature lonesome without its identical twin.

The next morning Simon didn't see Milena at her library desk. Paní Zrzavá's mother, she told Simon, had been taken to the hospital.

"Mother is all I've got." Paní Zrzavá's colorless lips twitched as she spoke.

She took Simon back to the reading room, where a bow-tied stork of a gentleman was examining a brittle-looking page through a magnifying glass. Simon sat at the other end of the oak table. Paní Zrzavá disappeared into the depths of the stacks. She returned with a brown box.

"This is Box Two," she said and let out a long sigh. "It's mostly family letters, photographs, medical records. But there are a few curious items, including, I believe, some notes for a story. Please be very careful. You're the first Western scholar to see these materials. Professor Cronin . . . Well, anyway, I should be going," she said.

Simon opened the box, feeling the same frenzy as the day before. He looked inside each of the folders and envelopes. He leafed through three photo albums, one from Gregor's childhood and high school years, one from his student years in Vienna, and one from Prague in the 1920s and '30s. There were also six large blue envelopes with letters from Gregor's parents, sister Adelina, and school and university friends.

The letters from each person were tied with twine and placed in smaller envelopes, on each of which Gregor wrote the years and the person's name: "Mother, 1916-1922," "Adi, 1920-1935," "Cousin Jiří, 1919-1937," and so forth. Simon wanted to go over the box's entire contents before starting to take notes.

At noon he ran downstairs to the library cafeteria, swallowed a cheese sandwich with a cup of acid-tasting coffee, and returned to the reading room. He had two files left to be examined. One turned out to be Gregor's diplomas and passport. The other—an envelope of poisonous green—was inscribed "Marienbad, 1937." Simon opened it, removing three postcards and some twenty pages of notes. Two postcards had been sent to Gregor at the spa town of Marienbad—one by his father, the other by his close friend Axel Freynt, who later wrote a memoir about Gregor. The third postcard was blank, unmailed. It was a color picture of a castle, reflected in a round lake and framed by verdure. The notes were written in German on the stationary of Pension Villa Magda, Marienbad. Simon spent the rest of the day euphorically deciphering Gregor's fluty handwriting.

It was a short story titled "The Jew's Castle." In 1933 the main character, a Jewish-Czech industrialist by the name of Arnošt Karolik, buys a castle in the mountains of Western Bohemia from an impoverished heiress to a family of Bohemian counts. Over the next two years he has the castle entirely renovated, and the moat and the pond cleaned. He liquidates all his businesses and deposits most of his money in Swiss banks. He settles down in the castle and hires half a dozen servants to attend to his needs and the needs of the horses and hunting dogs that he acquires for the estate. He starts throwing parties and inviting friends from Prague. He lives the life of an aristocrat, reveling in the fact that his wealth has finally made him the lawful owner of a castle. Only one thing is missing: he is an old bachelor without heirs.

Božena Lidová, a singer at the State Opera, visits Karolik at the castle about once a month, yet refuses to commit to marriage. In the meantime, more and more alarming signs reach Karolik from Germany. Here the reader starts wondering if Karolik hasn't gone mad. He orders large shipments of machine guns, grenades, and ammunition. He hires a small army from the local peasantry and trains them to defend his castle…

The story was left unfinished, interrupted in the middle of the page where Karolik's lover, the Czech soprano, begs him to abandon his "crazy idea" and leave the country "before it's too late."

Simon sat at the reading room until the closing hour. He walked across the Charles Bridge under a soft April shower. He loved everybody in Prague that evening: the young women who returned his probing looks; the blue-haired old ladies on the tram; the walrus-mustached, chesty metal workers walking to their pubs in groups of four or five. Vítek and Irenka were at home, and they invited Simon to join them and a group of friends for supper. They drove in the Chmelas' mosquito Citroen to a beer garden on the outskirts of the city. A group of ten people—former dissidents and their partners—sat around a long table, arguing politics and passing around fragrant joints. Simon sipped his beer, occasionally uttered a word or two. He was thinking of "The Jew's Castle."

The next morning Irenka didn't wake him up. It was a Saturday. The library was closed, and he decided to visit Felix Gregor's grave. Simon knew that Gregor was buried at Prague's New Jewish cemetery—as opposed to the ancient cemetery in the heart of Prague. He took a tram to the National Theater, then switched to another. The Jewish cemetery was next door to a large cemetery complex called Olšanské hřbitovy—a combination of both prewar and postwar burial grounds. The tram was full of older men and women and entire families; many were armed with gardening tools and carried flowers for planting. Simon was the only one to disembark at the stop for the Jewish cemetery. He found himself next to a tall arched stone entrance with cast iron gates and a low stucco and red-tile fence hugging the cemetery grounds. Beyond the main gate he saw a synagogue with a hipped roof and miniature, scimitar-shaped, dome on top.

The gates were closed. He peered inside and saw an old man, bony and hunched over, with disheveled gray hair waving in the cold wind. Dressed in a torn black jacket and brown pants, he was sitting in the sun on a crooked bench.

"Excuse me," Simon said in German. "I'd like to see the cemetery."

"*Das tut mir leid*," replied the old Czech guard. "The cemetery is closed. Come back tomorrow."

What was he thinking? Simon felt like a total idiot. Coming to visit a Jewish cemetery on a Saturday? He was so eager to see Gregor's grave that he didn't even think that the cemetery might not be open. Disparaging himself, Simon walked along the cemetery fence. Back in the Soviet Union, they used to sneak into parks after hours through secret entrances—loosened boards or bent iron bars in the fences. Looking across his shoulder to make sure no one could see him, Simon pulled at bar after bar in the synagogue fence until he found one detached from the bottom. He bent it just enough to slip in through the opening, stepping on a cushion of pressed leaves.

It took Simon over an hour to find the grave. It was part luck, part intuition. There were some rows where he checked every single gravestone, and some that he skipped entirely. Gregor's grave was at the far side of the cemetery, away from the synagogue. A simple basalt gravestone, an inscription in Czech: *"Felix Gregor Spisovatel 1900-1938."* The silver paint in the Star of David had lost its luster. A rowanberry tree was growing near the head of the grave. Simon photographed the gravestone and the surrounding area, put a chip of granite on the gravestone, and walked towards his secret entrance, a murmur of guilt radiating through his heart.

When he returned to Vítek and Irenka's house, he found a note taped to the side table in the room: "Telephone Milena." He dashed to the hallway phone and dialed the number in the note.

"That's you?" Milena's voice asked in disbelief.

"Milena, I looked for you at the library."

"I was home. I didn't feel well."

"Are you better now?"

"Now I'm well."

"I went to see Gregor's grave."

"I've never been there."

"What are you doing later today?" asked Simon.

"This evening?" Milena asked.

"Yes."

"Nothing. Rereading Gregor's stories."

"Would you like to go someplace together?"

"Yes."

"Good. We'll grab a bite together, and then, perhaps, you'll show me Prague."

They agreed to meet at the tram circle at seven.

Milena was already waiting near a newspaper kiosk when Simon got off the tram. He gave her a bunch of white daffodils. The flowers complimented Milena's outfit—a long black skirt with a yellow floral print and a black shirt under a white jacket.

"Beautiful," Simon said and took her hand—as easily as though they had been dating a long time.

"An American store just opened in Prague. I was nervous you wouldn't like my clothes."

As they walked across Charles Bridge, Simon thought of how stylish she looked—an ornate leather purse over her shoulder, daffodils in hand, her long hair, amber in the heedful light of the Prague sunset. In the middle of the bridge, Milena stopped and pointed to one of the bas-reliefs laid into the granite parapet. It was an image of a knight in armor. Milena took Simon's hand and pressed it to the casting, placing her own hand on top of his.

"This is what we do for good luck."

"Okay, good luck, then. Can we go to dinner at an elegant restaurant?"

Milena hesitated for a moment.

"Young people in Prague don't go to such places."

"It's my treat," said Simon. "Just for tonight let's pretend that we're not young people but established professionals."

"All right," Milena agreed. "Then I'll take you to a place where our elite go. Someone told me President Havel visits this place."

At the far side of the bridge they bumped into a tall young man with wavy hair arranged in a pony tail, dressed in black jeans and a matching denim jacket, and carrying a battered case with a musical instrument.

He greeted Milena with a pained smile.

"Frantík, *Jak se máš?*" Milena said and switched to English. "This is Simon. He's a researcher from America. Simon, this is Frantík."

Simon offered the Czech man a handshake, but he just nodded.

"See you around, Frantík," Milena said to the musician.

"Who is this guy?" Simon asked after they turned onto the embankment.

"My ex-boyfriend. He plays the clarinet."

"What's his problem?"

"Jealous. We were together for almost two years. And then I left him," Milena explained.

The last thing I need is a jealous Czech clarinetist, Simon thought to himself but didn't say anything.

They walked to a restaurant on the bank of the Vltava, with a view of the Castle up above. The lobby had velour furniture and marble statuettes. The musicians—a pianist, a saxophonist, a drummer, and a double bassist— wore white trousers and silver jackets. Simon ordered a bottle of champagne, a Caesar salad, and trout pâté.

"I recognize some famous people," Milena whispered to him.

"I only recognize one," Simon whispered back, leaning over and kissing her neck.

"That's a well-known operatic tenor," Milena explained, still speaking under her breath. "The women next to him is his wife, but everyone knows that he is a homosexual. And that one over there, he's a very good poet. He used to teach at Charles University but lost his job in 1978. Now he's teaching again. He has a new book about Ivan Blatný. Do you know Blatný?"

"No, tell me."

"He was a Czech poet who lived in a lunatic asylum in England after World War II. He mixed languages and wrote truly bilingual poems. Incredible."

Simon put her limp hand between his. "Most of the folks here look too . . . what should I say? . . . Posh," he said. "And not at all like artists or intellectuals."

"The new Czech bourgeoisie," Milena said. "They come here to rub elbows with real writers and artists. That's the way it used to be here before World War II. And that's the way it is again. A bohemian place."

"With a capital 'b'?" Simon joked.

"Both," Milena answered seriously.

"Do you think Gregor ever came here?" Simon asked.

A vigilant waiter removed their appetizer plates and refilled their flutes with champagne.

"No, I think he was too reclusive for that," Milena replied.

"Tell me, Milena, were Jews allowed here in the years before the Nazi occupation?" Simon asked.

Milena shook her head—as though indicating her embarrassment over his question.

"We didn't have a Jewish problem after 1918. It just was not an issue prior to the occupation. And Gregor, by the way, saw himself as a one-hundred-percent Czech."

"And that's why he wrote his prose in German?" Simon asked in a loud voice. Several people from the surrounding tables turned and regarded him with bemusement.

Milena rolled her palms over her cheeks. Then she replied: "Yes, this is true, but he wrote his poems in Czech, and they move me to tears as they do most other Czechs."

"My lovely Milena," Simon said after taking another sip of champagne. "I'm not implying that Gregor didn't feel at home here in Czechoslovakia. But he felt different. Not alien, but different. He was Czech, and he was also Jewish."

"I understand," Milena said in a subdued voice. "You probably think that someone who isn't Jewish cannot see the world the way a Jew does."

"An overstatement if there is one," Simon said with a chortle. "You, for instance, understand Gregor's fiction just as well as I do."

"For me," Milena replied, "Gregor is about pure fantasy. I don't think he was interested in Jewish affairs, Zionism, or any other kind of politics."

"Yes and no, Milena. You are right in that most of his stories are fantastical."

"Exactly. They are not about history."

"And yet," Simon said, excited. "And yet Jewish characters surface virtually in all of his works. And then there's something I found out just yesterday."

Milena regarded him silently.

"Tell me, please."

"There's this story Felix Gregor wrote in Marienbad in 1937. His last known work of fiction. It's in Box Two, unfinished. About a Jew who buys a castle from a former Bohemian countess."

"It's about Klara Rittenberg, isn't it?" Milena asked, clasping and unclasping her hands.

"It's about many things, and probably Klara is one of them. I'd like to investigate this further. It's his most militant story, that's for sure."

Silently they ate their éclairs and drank their coffee. Simon paid the bill in cash and they walked outside, where the wind had subsided and the air smelled of birdcherry blossoms. They silently strolled along the Vltava embankment for about ten minutes, holding hands. Then he kissed her. She kissed him back with lips alone, and then pressed her head to his chest. Guitar playing could be heard at a distance—students strumming and singing the Beatles at the Charles Bridge.

For the next two weeks Simon and Milena met every day after work and wandered around Prague until darkness. She took him to see her favorite neighborhoods and buildings. One of them was Bertramka, once the home of the Dušek family, where Mozart had courted a pretty young woman. It turned out that Milena adored Marina Tsvetaeva, the genius Russian poet who lived in Prague in the 1920s. She took Simon on a tour of Tsvetaeva's Prague residences, only one of which had a memorial plaque.

On a Sunday they finally visited the Old New Synagogue, which Simon had been avoiding, just as he stayed away from other tourist traps, and especially the ones guidebooks listed among a city's top sites. There was a small line of visitors, mainly Americans and Canadians, outside the squat ochre edifice with narrow windows and a rawboned gable. From a distance the synagogue looked like a boat, partly undressed after having been brought to a city wharf for reconditioning.

A handful of university-age boys and girls, who would have looked Jewish when surrounded by their West Slavic compatriots with pale eyes, ashen-blonde hair, pointy noses and raised cheek bones, stood outside the entrance and distributed paper *kippot* to the visitors.

A bespectacled girl inserted herself between Simon and Milena and asked, addressing Simon in an accented but fluent English:

"Are you a member of the Jewish community?"

Embarrassed, Simon replied: "I'm Jewish, if that's what you're asking. But I'm not a member." And for some reason he added, taking Milena's hand: "I'm from New Haven, Connecticut."

The bespectacled girl gave Milena a scornful look.

"Is the Golem's body still kept in the attic?" Simon asked.

"Oh that's a legend," the bespectacled girl answered, eyes widening.

As they entered the low ground floor, Milena pressed her head to Simon's shoulder and whispered,

"I've lived in Prague my whole life, but never been here."

Later that same day Milena took Simon to meet her friends Jarek and Katka, ex-hippies who were building a house in the outskirts of Prague. Jarek had a mane of rusty red hair and a patriarch's wiry beard. He wrote songs and made a living selling photographs of Prague to tourists. His partner, Katka, was what in America they might call "earthy": unshaved legs and armpits, long rainbow skirts, silver rings on many fingers and on big toes. She painted on ceramic plates of her own design, and Milena told Simon she never repeated herself. Katka's plates, which were exhibited and sold at a gallery in the old center, depicted everyday scenes of her city. The current of life Simon observed every day from the window of his tram on the way to the library and also in neighborhood pubs. Old ladies in kerchiefs making their grocery rounds; workers with large, bearded mugs of beer. There was also a series of plates with women in high heels standing under street lights. Simon thought the slight grotesqueness of Katka's painted scenes came less from the point of view than from the sheer mass of details.

When Jarek found out that Simon was doing research on Felix Gregor, he revealed that his own father was Jewish. Jarek's mother was Czech, and after the war his father started concealing his origins.

"Conceal would actually be the wrong word," Jarek explained to Simon as they sat drinking fruity white wine in the garden.

"How do you mean?" Simon asked.

"There would have been no repercussions for him, his name wasn't particularly Jewish, and it wasn't like in Stalin's Russia here. We had the Slansky trial in '52, but that was about all in the way of repressions against Jews."

Simon regarded him silently. As if reading his mind, Jarek said,

"And there weren't too many Jews left. Most of the ones who had survived later emigrated."

"Have you always known?" Simon asked.

"That I was a half-Jew?" Jarek returned the question. "Yes, but until I entered the university, I was quite ignorant of things Jewish."

When Simon and Milena were leaving, Jarek offered,

"If you want, I can take you around Smichov, where many Prague Jews lived before the war."

Three days later Jarek picked up Milena and Simon at the library, and they drove to Smichov, a district south-west of the old center. Simon had checked and confirmed that Gregor's birth certificate was missing in his papers, and the location of the house where his parents lived at the time of his birth was unknown. But he copied down the address where Gregor's parents lived in the 1920s until their death. As it turned out, it was only two blocks from a local synagogue erected in the 1860s. The synagogue's original building had been in the Moorish style, and one could still see crenellations on the roof and arched oriental windows in the upper row. It was rebuilt as a functionalist structure, a box with two rows of windows, the bottom ones with stained glass. There were Hebrew letters all along the façade, and beneath them, blocking the view of the entrance and the short pillars on which the front of the building rested, there was a vegetable store with an outside counter under a ripped green canopy. On the counter there were scales and wooden crates with potatoes, carrots, scallions, cabbage, and beets. A man wearing a dirty, white apron stood behind the counter, lazily talking with a customer. Local residents flitted by, checking out the wares and the prices. It was Wednesday afternoon, a quiet, sunny, breezy day, and everything looked as though it had always been that way—except for the simple fact that there was a vegetable store in the former synagogue. As Simon stood with Milena and Jarek in front of the synagogue where Gregor's parents probably used to pray, and where roots and tubers were now sold, he was thinking that Jarek, a child of a Jewish man and a non-Jewish woman, was himself like a vegetable store thrust into the former synagogue.

They went to a local café for lunch, after which Jarek dropped Simon and Milena off near the library. They walked across the Charles Bridge to the other side. It was four in the afternoon, and they had run out of sightseeing ideas. They stood near the tram circle, holding each other, unable to let go. Then they boarded a tram—his tram. Both could hardly speak on the way to Vítek and Irenka's house, first in the overstuffed car, later as they climbed to the top of the hill amid overgrown lilac shrubs and a fiefdom of wild flowers.

Standing in the middle of Simon's room—between the two beds—they kissed for a long time. Simon slipped his hand under her shirt, then the other hand, and felt the inverted clasp of her bra. He turned Milena around, pressing her back to his chest, kissing her neck and ears. He threw off his shirt, then helped Milena out of hers. She turned around, covering her breasts with both her hands.

"Can anybody hear us?" Milena asked.

"I don't know. It doesn't look like Vítek or Irenka are home."

She took his hand and led him to the bathroom, which was at the far end of his guest suite. There, standing between the shower stall and the sink, they kissed again. Milena's knees trembled, and she sat on the bathroom floor.

"I just can't here, lásko," she said. "I want you so much. But this rented room, strange people next door."

"Milena . . ." Simon was still trying to catch his racing breath. "This is what life is like. With small rooms and people next door. This is my home for the next few weeks."

They went back to the bedroom.

"Could we go away together?" Milena asked.

Simon didn't reply. He sat on the bed and took a fierce bite of a green apple. Milena's cheeks and forehead were febrile red.

"Can you please bring me some tea," she asked.

They drank tea in silence. Afterwards Simon walked Milena to the tram stop.

"When will I see you?" she asked, the side of her right hand sliding across his neck.

"At the library," he answered sternly. The arrival of the tram rescued them from an awkward pause.

Vítek was sitting in the garden when Simon came back. He was sipping tea out of an earthen mug.

"Now your life is in order," Vítek said and gave Simon a violent wink. "You're getting research done. You've got a Czech girlfriend. That's very good."

Simon looked up and saw a dense flock of birds fluttering across the sky. An April wedding of Czech starlings.

The following day Milena didn't come to work, and when he rang her in the afternoon, she said she was under the weather and had decided to take a couple of days off. That was all for the better, Simon thought to himself as he passed Milena's desk on the way to see Paní Zrzavá. The old spinster gave him a look of sheepish disapproval from under her thick lenses.

Simon and Milena didn't see each other over the weekend.

On the Monday of his fourth week in Prague Simon woke up at five and was unable to go back to sleep. He was missing a piece of information in his research, and he lay awake, listening to the squabble of birds and going over— in his head—the contents of Gregor's archive. There were two questions to which Simon felt he still hadn't found the answers. They were related, these questions. One was about Nazism. In all of the letters that had been published, including those to his sister Adelina, who was living in Paris after 1936, Gregor made no mention of the Nazi aggression and the impending catastrophe. Was he in denial, like many fellow Central European Jews? The other question concerned Countess Klara Rittenberg. Simon knew from the volume published by Klara's nephews, that in March of 1937 Gregor returned all Klara's letters with a tortured note, composed in German: "I know, my love, that I'm no less Czech than you, whose ancestors had been living in these lands since the tenth century. But let's face it: even though they no longer have noble titles here, I am and always will be a Jew, and you a countess."

Klara Rittenberg emigrated to Switzerland in the spring of 1937. In May of 1937 Gregor went to take the cure in the West Bohemian spa triangle, and he didn't come back to Prague until September of the same year. Sometime during the summer he started "The Jew's Castle." Could it be that he wrote it while staying in Marienbad? Simon mused. Already after having returned the letters to Klara? Something in this chain of events troubled him, like a missing link. And this link had to do with Klara. How could she just acquiesce and leave after Gregor's farewell note? Simon kept asking himself. There was something wretchedly flat in that finale.

At the library, he settled into his chair in the reading room and examined his notes. Then he went through all the materials in boxes One and Two of Gregor's papers, making sure he hadn't missed anything of significance. He checked his notes against the letters and manuscripts he had copied down in longhand. Box Three had been of little interest to him. He checked out Gregor's medical records, including a note, written by a spa physician in Marienbad, and prescribing alkaloid mineral water, long walks three times a day, lots of fish and fresh greens. There were also Gregor's books with notes and corrections in the margins, usually the bread and butter of a textualist, often the tedium of a biographer. Simon was at an impasse, and he forced himself to spend the rest of the day reviewing Gregor's marginalia—just to rule out a hidden clue.

He started with the prose. By lunchtime he had gone through a dozen periodicals with Gregor's stories, as well as Gregor's novellas and only novel. The corrections were mostly minor—typos, a verb here and a noun there; nothing to get excited about. Simon took a break and ate a grilled lamb chop with salad and a glass of beer. After lunch he moved to a little café next door, read the *Tribune*, had a piece of cheesecake with Turkish coffee. The morning's anxiety was almost gone. He wasn't finding anything new. *Na net i suda net,* he thought to himself in Russian. This joyfully illogical saying literally meant "there's no judgment when the answer is no." Simon slowly strolled back and bumped into Milena on the steps of the library.

She was back at work and taking a late lunch break. Simon offered to accompany her. He told her about his search for something related to Klara Rittenberg. It was sunny and warm outside, the final week of April. A breeze from the Vltava carried the humid scent of Slavic spring. The awkwardness of the past week had evaporated, and they chatted with the same ease and enchantment as during the first days. Simon was going back to finish with Box Three. They agreed to meet outside around five and spend the evening together. Running up the three long flights of stairs, Simon felt the giddiness of the first Prague weeks easing back into his body.

He looked through three more collections with Gregor's contributions, still finding nothing of substance. One thing was missing: Gregor's poetry collections. Simon went to look for Paní Zrzavá. She was not at her desk, and he sat and waited, staring at her family photos in chipped oval frames.

When Paní Zrzavá finally came back, she was hiding her hands in the deep pockets of her worn-out smock.

"Why didn't you send for me?" she asked. "I was in the depository downstairs." A cobweb was stuck in Paní Zrzavá's thin hair.

"I don't mind waiting," Simon replied.

"What is your question?" Paní Zrzavá asked, as though she meant for him to leave her alone.

"I was wondering what happened to Gregor's poetry volumes. The rest of his publications are all in the box."

"You cannot see them," said the old archivist.

"Why not, Paní Zrzavá?"

"The pages are too brittle. The books have to be sent to preservation. And there's something else too. It involves copyright matters. Dr. Seifertová will be making that determination," said Paní Zrzavá, wiping her glasses with the lap of her black coat.

"I don't understand, Paní Zrzavá. What copyright matters? These poems have been reprinted many times. I only wish to see if Gregor left any notes or corrections."

"That's not the issue," the old lady said.

"So what is the issue, then?" Simon was losing his patience.

"It's something else, something private."

"Private?" Simon asked.

"Yes. Very."

"Paní Zrzavá, with all due respect, I was given complete access to Gregor's archive."

"*Gospodin* Reznikov." Paní Zrzavá's lips started trembling. She addressed him with the Russian word for "mister." "*Gospodin* Reznikov, you are very pushy, aren't you?"

Here it finally comes, Simon thought. The pushy Jew stuff. It's taken her awhile.

"It must be your past. The Soviet invasiveness, the sort that my poor mother still fears even worse than the German discipline."

"No, Paní Zrzavá," Simon replied slowly and quietly. "It's also my American present. And my Jewish everything."

"That's a taboo subject," Paní Zrzavá cut him off. "And don't even think of accusing me of prejudice. My father was a Jew."

"I'm merely trying to get to the bottom of things," Simon said. "I came all the way to Prague for this, and I still don't know what you mean by 'very private.'"

"I'll need to clear this with the director. Dr. Seifertová is away until next week at an international congress of librarians in Budapest."

"Paní Zrzavá, please," Simon intoned.

"You may complain to the director when she is back in the office. And she'll probably overrule me in order to please the esteemed American visitor. But until then—over my dead body."

"Paní Zrzavá, we wouldn't want you dead." Simon forced out the joke.

On the way out he said to Milena: "The old bat wouldn't budge."

"Excuse me, Simon," Milena asked. "The old bat wouldn't what?"

"Wouldn't let me see the Czech poetry collections," Simon said, impatience in his voice.

"Maybe she'll change her mind," Milena said, tucking a loose braid behind her ear. "She's a kind soul."

Stringing together in his head the tired clichés about heart and soul, Simon felt trapped in a no-man's-land that separated his Soviet past and his American present. Ambition had brought him to Prague, and now his expedition had come to a halt. But Milena—was she too part of this research mission? Simon asked himself.

That night Simon had insomnia again, tossing in his narrow bed. There were no screens on the windows, and he kept getting up—now to slam the windows shut, now to let in daybreak's blackcurrant air. He had finally sunk into a bottomless sleep when the garden came alive with chirrups and trills; and by the time he sat down outside to have his breakfast, Irenka'a pancakes were cold and sticky. Simon spread on the homemade jam and ate them, chasing each bite with a sip of tepid, strong tea.

He didn't get to the library until after ten in the morning, and Milena wasn't at her desk. Simon opened his notebook and closed it. There was nothing left for him to do, and he decided to see Paní Zrzavá again and plead with her one more time.

Instead of the old archivist, he found Milena sitting at her cluttered desk.

"Didn't expect to find you here," Simon said. "Where's the old bat?"

"It's her mother . . . she had to miss work."

"Why do you sound so mysterious?"

"Close your eyes," Milena said to Simon.

"Why?"

"You'll see."

Simon felt something like a piece of cardboard rubbing against the knuckles of his right hand. He opened his eyes and saw an old envelope, which Milena held in her cupped hands.

"I'll probably get in trouble for this, but we only live once," Milena said with a particular brightness in her voice.

"Milena?" Simon asked in disbelief.

"Gregor's poetry collections. Paní Zrzavá kept them in her desk. Hurry, Simon, we'll talk at the end of the day."

Simon ran back to the reading room. He untied the twine crisscrossing the envelope and pulled out three little volumes. The first one, published in 1925 in Prague, had no corrections, and he soon put aside its scrawny, yellowed body. The second was illustrated by another Czech Jew, Josef Kuh, and contained about a dozen corrections and Gregor's drawing of a hippopotamus on the title page. The last volume, Simon's favorite of all three, bore the title *Poems before Dawn*. Published in the Moravian capital, Brno, in 1935, it was the slimmest of the three collections. Simon leafed through the pages, finding a few corrected typos. The poem on page seventeen bore a dedication: "To K. R." Glued in between pages seventeen and eighteen was a slender milky-white envelope. Simon turned the book over and helped a letter on monogrammed paper out of the envelope. Unlike Klara's other letters Simon had read, this one was written not in German but in Czech. His first impulse was to ask Milena for help, but this would have exposed her. He had to do it on his own, and it took Simon over an hour to figure it out and translate it into English:

27 March 1937

My Dear Gregor,

Your note and the returned letters affected me so profoundly that I was physically unable to respond straightaway. But now I am feeling stronger, and spring is finally here after this awful protracted winter.

I beg you to read this letter very carefully as ~~every word,~~ every comma here yearns for your understanding. You write that we cannot be together because you are the son of a Jewish pharmacist and I the daughter of a Bohemian count. You have said this before and during our previous separations, and my answer has not changed. I love you as you are and for the person you are, and all I ask is for you to do the same.

Gregor, my dear-dear Gregor, I could fill pages with loving words about your writing—the only writing that I adore and consume with passion. I could tell you about the way my whole being aches for you. But this is not the time to do it, and

I think you know it already. Gregor, evil times are upon us. The darkness is moving eastward and will soon swallow up our country and European civilization. Come away with me, my love. We'll be married and live in Switzerland together. (Or, perhaps, we should move to America?) What's mine will be yours. We don't even have to get married if you don't wish to. I implore you to put aside your pride and trust me with your future. I kiss you. I love you.

Next week I'm going to Sion and will be staying at my aunt's until I have made further arrangements. I await your reply.

With all my love and devotion,

Yours, as ever,

Klara

Simon copied down the letter, reread his own translation twice, making small corrections, and returned the original to the envelope. He stared aimlessly at the stained-glass window until the bells started chiming. It was five o'clock. Milena was waiting downstairs.

"You look upset, what's wrong?" she asked after they kissed.

"Nothing. Everything. I'll tell you in a minute."

Milena put her hand in his as they headed for the bar where they had had drinks on their first date.

"I've just read the most amazing letter from Klara. She wrote it in March 1937—before Gregor went to Western Bohemia. She offered to take him to Switzerland."

"But he didn't go. What does it mean?" Milena asked.

"He gets this letter from Klara, and in May he goes to Marienbad. And then some time during the summer he writes 'The Jew's Castle.' I can feel a connection. Now I've got to visit the places where Gregor stayed that summer."

"May I accompany you on the trip?" Milena asked, solicitously.

"I'd love it if you came."

They sat outside until dark, sipping tart red wine and making plans for their expedition to the Bohemian spa triangle.

Two days later, at around three in the afternoon, Simon picked up Milena at their usual meeting spot. He had had quite a bit of trouble locating a car rental place on his side of town. It was the long holiday weekend commemorating May 1, International Workers' Day, which they still celebrated in the Czech Republic. Eventually, and through Irenka's assistance, Simon found a local garage that rented him a veteran Škoda. It had the tightest of clutches and vibrated like a power drill when going over sixty kilometers an hour.

It took them over three hours to get to Marienbad, or Mariánské Lazně, as the spa was called in Czech. They stopped in Plzeň—Simon was curious to see the breweries. They also paused to visit a castle built on the top of a mountain, below which, in a gorge, a black river meandered amid mossy banks. Hops grew all along the two-lane highway, and Milena explained that every fall Czech students went to harvest them.

"In Russia students were forced to pick potatoes," Simon remarked with theatrical solemnity. "And here you guys pick hops. Therein lies the difference between Russian lands and Czech lands."

"Because Czechs drink beer," Milena said, laughing the happiest of laughs, "And Russians drink vodka."

"Except now I drink scotch."

"You're American. And believe it or not, I've never tried scotch or whiskey. Just read about it in Hemingway's stories."

"You can try it in Marienbad," said Simon. "They've got to have normal bars and restaurants."

Milena didn't reply.

Outside the window, Bohemian landscapes rolled on. The fields had just been plowed, and they looked like wet, brown roofs. Wooded hillocks framed the view on both sides of the highway. The smells of malt, silage, and freshly mowed grass mixed in the evening air. Arriving in Marienbad was like entering the past. The moonlit, Empire-style façades; angels and maidens on the roofs; chestnut trees everywhere. Milena and Simon drove around, mesmerized by the emptiness of the streets, the quietude, the elegant villas and hotels. They checked out two pensions but didn't like the rooms. Then they inquired at a hotel called Villa Victoria and took a top-floor room with a view of the main square and the spa colonnade. The room had dark parquet floors and carved mahogany furniture. It cost about forty dollars.

"An American graduate student is rich in Marienbad," Simon said to Milena.

They went out to look for a restaurant. Walking on the town's main boulevard, they paused to read the menus—sometimes posted outside, and sometimes obtained from a reluctant maitre d'.

"You don't sound like an American when you try to speak Czech," Milena said. "If you did, you would get better service. They think you're from Russia."

"Good. Let them think whatever they wish, my Czech princess."

"Say it again," Milena asked.

"My beautiful Czech princess," Simon repeated, first in English, then in Czech. "*Moje krásná, česká princezno.*"

They ate in a restaurant just steps from the spa colonnade. Only two tables were occupied when they went in. The dining room could easily have seated two hundred people. Simon ordered a bottle of German sparkling wine, earning nods of approval from a tall waiter with large, hirsute ears. The bottle arrived, cocooned in a silver bucket.

The consommé came with a whole dropped egg and meat patties on the side. For the main course Milena ordered braised rabbit, and Simon the local specialty—roasted carp, which in Czech is called *kapr*. A drunk Czech fisherman must have switched around the letters the letters, Simon thought to himself. When the bill came, Simon discovered that they had been charged separately for bread, lemon, and sugar. No matter, he was happy to pay the extra pennies. He even found endearing the waiters' thespian slowness, the overcooked entrées, and the lifeless jazz band.

They strolled a bit up and down the boulevard, then stopped for a drink at an outdoor bar, where three German businessman were discussing the physical merits of Czech women. Milena hated her scotch, and Simon ended up drinking it along with his own, ordering her a cherry liqueur instead.

"I miss Europe," Simon suddenly said.

"You do?"

"It's hard to explain. . . . I haven't been back to Russia since we left, but what I miss in America is a certain European charm."

"My father went to Russia on business," Milena said. "He felt like he was in an alien territory."

"I'm not surprised. Here it feels a lot more like Western Europe. Reminds me of Vienna, where I got my first taste of freedom."

"Prague is actually further west than Vienna," Milena said with pride.

"I know, I know. But it's not really the distance . . ."

"You're an American guy now," Milena said, letting her right hand brush against his right check. "I don't think of you as Russian."

"That's funny," said Simon. "In America they usually think of me as Russian. That I'm Jewish is often an afterthought . . ."

Back at the hotel, past midnight, Milena slipped into the shower, and Simon waited, sitting on the wide windowsill and staring at the dark, bumpy roofs upon which silver cherubs stood watch. Cicadas chirped. Milena was humming an R.E.M. song. She finally came out of the bathroom, a towel wrapped around her body, wet hair glistening in the room's semi-darkness.

"Here I am." She walked toward him.

"Milena, Milena," Simon muttered as she helped him out of his clothes.

After Simon rolled off to his side of the bed, Milena kissed him on the clavicle and whispered,

"I don't know where I am."

After breakfast Milena and Simon went down to reception to ask about the location of Villa Magda, where Gregor had stayed. The proprietor, a ruddy gentleman in a burgundy, knitted vest, had never heard of either a pension by that name or the writer Felix Gregor.

"Many names changed after the war," he said. "You should talk to Jan Bartoš."

"Who's Jan Bartoš?" Simon asked, a little annoyed.

"He's a journalist," Milena explained. "Writes the society column for *Reflex*. It's a popular tabloid."

"Mr. Bartoš is down here for the weekend, covering the consecration of a new curative spring," the proprietor added. "The local bishop is coming. Tomorrow there'll be a ceremony and an outdoor mass at the colonnade."

"And how do we find this Mr. Bartoš?" Simon asked.

"He's up in his room now. Number 407."

A slender woman in black, leather pants and a red, cotton shirt let them in. Bartoš was a grasshopper of a man with hazel beady eyes that lingered on the faces of the people with whom he spoke. When Bartoš heard that the matter concerned Felix Gregor, his nostrils flared rhythmically like those of a pointer sniffing the air.

"I didn't know he stayed here. Very interesting," he said. "For how long?"

"The summer of 1937," Simon replied, feeling ambushed. "You can actually read about it in Axel Freynt's book. It's translated into Czech and came out here."

"I know German," Bartoš stated, looking past Milena and Simon. "So how can I be of help to you?"

"If you were researching a local story and needed to locate an old, possibly renamed building, what would you do?" Simon asked.

"Very simple." Bartoš lit a cigarette and continued. "You go to the local historical museum and ask to see the architectural plans. Almost every town has those, most certainly the spa towns."

The Town Museum was halfway between their hotel and the spa colonnade. A Greek revival building, it smelled of stone dust and old newsprint. The museum clerk had an oxblood perm and wore a dress suit of the sort Simon's maternal grandmother, a trade union functionary, used to wear when Simon was a child in Moscow. The old lady became more and more agitated with each of the questions Milena translated from English into Czech:

"Have you heard of Villa Magda?"

"Villa Magda?"

"Is there a prewar city plan we could see?"

"A prewar plan? Only Herr Direktor would be able to help you. All the guides and city plans are kept in his office," the museum clerk replied.

"Where is Herr Direktor?" Milena and Simon asked simultaneously.

"Having lunch with his family."

"Could he be contacted?" Simon pressed.

"Herr Direktor does not like to be disturbed on a Saturday," the old clerk said, switching to German.

"Please, this is very important, and Mr. Reznikov is only here for today," Milena added, stroking the museum clerk's stooped back.

The old lady made a telephone call and told them to wait. In a few minutes a pimply youth appeared, dressed in a white, oversized shirt and a tight striped vest. He tried to speak English, but soon gave up. He said that he would run to Herr Direktor's apartment and explain that "an important foreign visitor" was waiting.

"He is a very kind man, our Herr Direktor," said the pimply youth. "I'm sure he will help you. Wait here."

The youth in the striped vest returned in about fifteen minutes.

"Herr Direktor knows you're here," he said. "He's on his way."

They waited for half an hour. Finally a short, bearded man in jeans and a sports coat of ocher tweed walked through the door and greeted Milena and Simon with energetic, double handshakes.

"Michal Rakovník," he introduced himself. "Please, to my office."

The office was cluttered with books, maps, bronze busts, and stuffed birds. The walls were decorated with sabers and duel pistols.

"So let's see, you're writing about Felix Gregor," the director said, speaking fast in English. "One of my favorites."

"Any help you can give us would be great," Simon said.

The director summoned the pimply youth and asked him to make coffee and fetch some fresh pastries from the bakery next door. While the youth was gone, the director gave them a quick overview of the museum's collections and a brief sketch of his own career. Talking a mile a minute—now in Czech, now in English—he explained that he had gone to school for geology, and in the

1970s had ended up working in Marienbad as a city geologist, later inheriting the director's job.

"Things used to be quiet here. Dead quiet," the director said as he poured the coffee. "Please, these are very good," he said, pointing to fruit tarts arranged on a porcelain tray. "Now it's a different story. German tourists. Ladies of the night. Money. It's a rare occasion to have interesting visitors like you."

"Mr. Rakovnik, here's the situation," Simon said. "Gregor spent a summer in Marienbad in 1937. We know from his letters that he stayed at a pension called Villa Magda. I'd like to find it."

"Piece of cake. Just give me a few minutes," said the director and disappeared into an adjacent room. He soon returned with a folio-size tome.

"This is the *Kurliste*. The tourist office used to publish it here until 1949. This is the 1937 volume. Let's see here." The director bit on the nail of his short middle finger and started leafing through the index. "Aha, here you go. Gregor, Felix, two entries. Getting warmer."

"Why two?" Simon asked, getting up from his deep leather chair. Milena also got up.

"That we shall find out momentarily. Let's go first to page 783."

The director turned to a page that was divided into five columns, and read the entry, translating it from German. "Gregor, Felix, single, permanently residing in Prague, Pension Villa Magda, checked in on May 19."

"That's it," Simon exclaimed. "Villa Magda. How can we get the address?"

"I'll check the prewar town plans. But let us first take a look at the second entry."

"Why would there be a second entry?" Simon asked in disbelief. "We know he stayed at Villa Magda. He wrote a story on its stationery. He also sent letters to his parents, friends, and his sister Adi. They all say Hotel Magda on the letterhead."

"Patience, my young colleague. Patience. Let's see. . . . Page 807. Here it is: Gregor, Felix, single, permanently residing in Prague, Hotel Aglaja, checked in on August 7."

"Hotel Aglaja? Where's that?"

The director disappeared again and came back with a leather portfolio and several books. He became engrossed in the search.

"We shall first look up the two hotels in these guide books to the entire spa area. I've got one from 1935, one from 1955, and a recent one. Okay, here we go. Pension Magda, Ibsenova ulice, which means Ibsen Street—Ibsen must have stayed here, that's a joke of course—number 27. Very well, I shall now look up this number on the city plan."

The director removed several maps and plans from the portfolio and unfolded them on his desk, pushing his coffee cup to the side.

"Here, let's see. I believe the buildings have been renumbered . . ."

After consulting city plans and guide books, they determined that in the 1950s Villa Magda had merged with an expanded hotel next door, Hotel Lev, when both were being renovated. The new street number was 175. But with the other hotel, the one where Gregor stayed after moving out of Villa Magda, things were more complicated. Gregor never mentioned the other place in his letters. In the 1950s Hotel Aglaja was renamed Hotel Zátiší, which literally meant Hotel "Quiet Place." It was about five kilometers outside Marienbad. The director photocopied for them a description from the 1935 travel guide that advertised "quiet country living, simple hearty meals, walks in the forest."

Simon looked at his watch: it was almost four o'clock. They had three hours before sunset. Following a map that Rakovník had xeroxed for them, they first walked to Ibsen Street and located number 175. The hotel was a section of a five-story stucco building, painted magenta. Statues of two women in togas stood on either side of the door. Doric columns went up between the second and fourth floor. They inquired at the front desk if they could see one of the top-floor rooms. The receptionist, who was doing her nails, eagerly gave them a key to a vacant room facing the town's central square.

"There are eight rooms on each floor," she explained. "Four facing each side."

In one of the letters from that summer Gregor mentioned having a fifth-floor room with a view of the town. Simon opened the windows. Across the rooftops they could see parts of the main square, the roof of the colonnade, and wooded hills for miles around. A road curved and uncurved around the foothills, disappearing in the emerald treetops. To the left, across the courtyard, they saw the bronze roof of another hotel, and two female figures crowning two dormers—each of the figures standing on a metal globe. One held a laurel wreath in her right hand, and with her left she pressed to her lips a long, thin bugle. The second bronze woman was holding a laurel wreath in her left hand; in her right hand, lowered behind her back, she had a paint brush.

"Milena said, "These muses are blaring promises of fame. Now I can see why Gregor liked it here."

"The question is: Why did he move out?" Simon pronounced pensively.

He took photos, first from the room, then from the street. They rushed back to the hotel, got into the car, and drove west in the direction of the country hotel that was once called Hotel Aglaja.

They turned onto a narrow road. Fir trees on opposite sides locked their branches in furious handshakes. Milena was looking on the left, Simon on the right. They passed two boys on bicycles. Their bamboo fishing poles were tied to the bicycles' frames. The boys waved at them and made funny faces.

"Let's ask them, Milena," Simon suggested.

They waited for the boys to catch up with them. Milena asked the older one how to get to Hotel Zátiší.

"Zátiší? My mother works there as a receptionist. Turn right after the road bends. There's a big stone on the left side of the road."

The stone was overgrown with red lichen. There was no sign pointing to the hotel, just a gravel path darting off to the right. They saw a three-storied Tudor-style mansion with the sign "Zátiší" and the words "Hotel" and "Vinárna" painted on either side of the sign.

The lobby smelled of dumplings and gravy. A boor's head with disconsolate eyes hung over the reception desk. A young cleaning lady was washing the floors on her hands and knees. Two little girls, chased by an old grandmother in a sundress and a gauze kerchief, cavorted past them across the lobby.

They hit the bell and a receptionist with two front gold teeth came out of the office. She was eating a green apple.

"We are all full up, I'm sorry," she said and burst out laughing.

"We just wanted to check the place out," Milena explained. "A writer by the name of Felix Gregor stayed here in 1937. The hotel was still called Hotel Aglaja back then."

"Never heard of a Felix Gregor. The hotel was renamed after the war," said the receptionist and wiped the corners of her mouth with the back of her fleshy hand.

"We were just wondering if it's possible to take a quick look around," Milena asked. "The foreign visitor would like to know what Mr. Gregor saw around here. He had asthma, and his doctor told him to take regular walks."

As they were walking out, the receptionist yelled: "Check out the pond. And the hunting lodge. A short walk through the forest."

They followed a path that began a few steps from the front porch. The path was laden with last year's fir needles. The survivors, tercentenarian beeches, rustled through their memories. The path brought Milena and Simon to a clearing with dark brown circles of burned-out grass. Through the openings in hazel shrubs on the far side of the clearing, the pond showed its shimmering tin surface. With the exception of a lane that must have been cleared for swimming, the entire side of the pond was studded with yellow water lilies. A pair of swans glided through the water.

A small castle, surrounded by overgrown elms and thickets of willows, stood on the other side of the pond. It was a two-storied structure, probably built around the 1900s in that fairytale Gothic style that was temporarily in vogue across Europe. Laid out in greenish granite, the castle had curtain walls with arrow holes and two symmetrical watch towers. The gaping windows, as well as the boarded-up entrance, suggested that the structure hadn't been in use. A second castle trembled before them on the surface of the water. Double carp ambled across vitreous water.

"This is it!" Simon said. "Gregor's castle. I'm sure of it! This all makes sense. He must have been taking a long walk and come upon this place. He liked it so much that he took a room at the former Hotel Aglaja. They didn't have their own stationery, so he continued to use the stationery of Pension Magda."

"So you think he started 'The Jew's Castle' here?" Milena asked.

"Pretty sure."

"He saw the hunting lodge, imagined buying it and moving into it?" Milena asked.

"I think I'm in love with you, Milena," Simon said and took both her hands.

"You think or you are?" asked Milena.

"I know I'm in love with you," Simon corrected himself.

She put her arms around his neck and kissed him, very slowly and tenderly.

"Milena, would you ever consider leaving Prague?" Simon asked, surprised by his unrehearsed question.

"I would only leave my country if I found absolute love," Milena replied, pronouncing the whole sentence like an incantation.

She wouldn't stop smiling even after they got back to the car.

In the morning, after a breakfast heavy on meat and cheese and light on fruit, they paid a second visit to Michal Rakovník's office at the Town Museum. The director again disappeared into the back room and brought out a stack of leather-bound tomes and a few smaller books. After what had happened the day before at the country hotel, Simon wasn't even too surprised when the director told them that the little castle had been built by Klara's uncle, Count Otto Rittenberg, in the 1900s.

"I think I understand what happened." Simon spoke fast, turning now to Milena, now to Rakovník. "They saw each other here for the last time. She came from Switzerland and stayed at her family lodge. He arranged to be at the nearby hotel. This way they could see each other as much as they wanted to—away from the public eye. And the unfinished story was Gregor's reply to Klara."

"A farewell?" Milena asked.

"Yes, but also a warning," Simon answered.

"Brilliant," Rakovník said and shook Simon's hand.

He lit up his cherry pipe with a match, took a few puffs, and then spoke again. "They were unusual, these Rittenbergs, and Klara Rittenberg was the most unusual of the whole lot."

"What happened to the castle after Klara emigrated?" Milena asked.

"Ah, spoils of history," the director replied. "After the war the place was nationalized, and an orphanage for sick children was opened here. It closed in the 1960s because of a lack of funding. Later there were plans to turn the castle into a museum of local Bohemian history, but until a few years ago there were more castles and palaces around here than there were visitors." The director released a cloud from his pipe. "But that may change now that we're back in Europe. Who knows?"

They took Rakovník out to lunch. Afterwards, he walked them to the car and even bought yellow tulips for Milena.

"Come visit again," he said as they were getting into the car. "Many Russian writers have stayed here. Gorky, Khodasevich, Nabokov . . ."

Leaning on an old lamppost, Rakovník waved until he merged with charcoal tree trunks and green benches in the rearview mirror.

The week after Milena and Simon's return to Prague from Marienbad was the happiest week of their love. Simon was done with his research. As he put finishing touches to his notes, he felt the story of Gregor's life literally changing before his eyes.

He saw Milena every day. They had lunch and supper together, and every night they were out till late. They didn't speak of the future.

Thursday evening Milena took him home to meet her family. Her father, who had done well for himself after the Velvet Revolution, selling German agricultural supplies, had bought and rebuilt a mansion in what was now a far suburb east of Prague. After greeting Simon, he handed him a bottle of beer and took him on a tour of his vegetable garden. He was a bear of a man, with a red, permanently sunburned face, graying copper hair, and big hands with silvery palms. He asked Simon if his parents had a garden and was pleased to hear that his father grew tomatoes and cucumbers in the backyard of their house in a Boston suburb.

"In the spring my father and I have a ritual. We go to farmer's market, buy tomato and cucumber plants, and plant them together," Simon explained.

"I grow mine out of seeds, my own seeds," Milena's father said proudly, spreading his heavy arms.

Milena came out of the house, where she had been helping her mother fix a meal, and stood on the porch, listening to her father and Simon. Later Simon met Milena's brother, a tall handsome teenager with a pony tail. All the furniture looked brand new, as though it had been purchased at the same time. Milena's mother, who used to work at a kindergarten, was wearing an apron over a denim skirt and a pink T-shirt.

Simon had been picturing a boisterous father and a pious mother—both asking him if he had serious intentions regarding their daughter. But Milena's parents didn't ask him any such questions. After supper Milena took him to see her room on the second floor of the house. She had white furniture, which made him think of a girl's bedroom in a middle-class American home. Hanging on the walls was a Modigliani poster and another one by a Czech artist of whom Simon had never heard. Simon thought: Four weeks ago we spoke for the first time, and now I'm sitting on Milena's bed and looking through her childhood photo albums.

When he followed Milena outside, it was chilly, cloudy, with no stars visible in the sky. Their hands clasped, they stepped down from the porch into the front yard. Milena led him on a walk across a nearby field, which gave out a scent of warming earth. A familiar, Slavic scent, Simon thought to himself.

"My mother said you had a lot of space inside," Milena said when they got into her mother's red Audi. "She said it was important in a relationship."

They were driving back to Prague on an empty road.

"And what did you father say about me?" Simon asked.

"He's a man of few words when it comes to this. Imagine, I had already been dating Frantík for a year, and he finally asked if he was treating me nicely."

"That's long time," Simon commented. He was tempted to ask more about Milena's ex-boyfriend but hesitated. Instead he said, a bit glibly, "My father doesn't hold back. Nor does my mom. I sometimes fear their verdict."

They talked of many things that night outside the gate of Vítek and Irenka's house. Their parting was only a few days away, and they found refuge in recollecting the hours and days they had shared. Milena brought up their trip to Western Bohemia, the gnomish museum director at Marienbad. They both laughed with relief, recalling the empty restaurant and the waiters' chessboard servility.

Simon glanced at his watch; it was past eleven. He asked Milena to stay over, expecting that she wouldn't, but she agreed. They parked her car next to Vítek's, and then walked on tiptoes into the main part of the house, so Milena could call home . . .

In the morning, when they came out into the garden, the table was set for two, and Irenka greeted Milena as if she and Simon had always been together. She sat and drank tea with them, chatting with Milena in Czech about mutual acquaintances they found almost instantly, including a clarinetist who was her ex-boyfriend's teacher at the State Music Conservatory, and about things Simon had never heard Milena speak of before: shoes, makeup, hair stylists. After breakfast Simon and Milena drove to the center. Milena left the car near the Vltava embankment, where she sometimes parked when she took her mother's car into town. They walked hand in hand to the library, running into Paní Zrzavá on the echoing staircase. She turned her face to the wall.

"Now she really hates me," Simon said to Milena.

"She thinks that men are out to hurt women," Milena explained. "Unless the men are geniuses like Felix Gregor. Then she takes the men's side."

"Is that why she detests Klara Rittenberg?" Simon asked.

That Friday was Simon's last day at the library. He and Dr. Seifertová had coffee in her smoky office, and he gave her a report, including an account of the Marienbad trip. She chuckled at his description of the visit to the Town Museum and wrote down the name of Michal Rakovník.

"He sounds intelligent. I should get in touch with him," she said, letting out a whirl of bluish smoke.

They talked about the possibility of Simon's translating and publishing "The Jew's Castle" in America. Gregor had no direct heirs, and the issue of rights was a little complicated. When Simon was getting up to leave, she stopped him with a gesture of her mannish hand.

"I heard you had a little falling out with our good old Paní Zrzavá," she said.

"I wouldn't call it a 'falling-out,'" Simon answered, vaguely. "We just see things a little differently."

"I want you to know that she was the one who discovered Gregor's boxes in a storage vault under piles of old newspapers and rubbish. So, naturally, she regards Gregor's archive with . . . what should I say? . . . a protective eye. Please remember to thank her before you take your leave."

"I fully intend to do that, *Paní Renato*."

"We all have high hopes for your book," said the director of the library, shaking and holding on to his hand.

"Not yet a book, only a dissertation," Simon replied.

"But it will be an important book," said Dr. Seifertová.

They said goodbye, and Simon went to look for Paní Zrzavá, but only found a rumpled lacy handkerchief on her desk. He was relieved that he wouldn't have to face her again. On a postcard he had bought to send to his parents in Boston, Simon wrote her a note in Russian, asking her "to forgive my insolence." He also left a little note on Milena's desk, asking to meet him at "our wine bar at 6."

Walking from Klementinum towards the Charles Bridge, Simon thought of how soothing it felt to be an anonymous person in a seething city crowd. His plane was leaving Saturday morning, and Friday was their last day together in Prague. His original plan had been to do some souvenir shopping and find a present for his mother, perhaps a locally made scarf or shawl or a pair of earrings with Czech garnets. Instead, without fully knowing what he was doing, he hopped on the tram. From his stop he ran up the hill all the way to

Vítek and Irenka's house. He borrowed Vítek's portable Consul, its slaten body reminding him of his own father's old typewriter. Kneeling in front of the only chair in his room, Simon machine-gunned the text of an invitation:

Simon Reznikov
516 Whitney Avenue, Apt. 2
New Haven, CT 06511 USA

The US Consulate
Prague, Czech Republic

It is my pleasure to invite Ms. Milena Krupičková, citizen of ⌐the Czech Republic *Czechoslovakia, to visit me in the United States of America during June–August 1993. Ms. Krupičková is a close friend of mine, and the purpose of her visit will be tourism. Throughout the duration of Ms. Krupičková's stay in the United States I will take care of her accommodations and, if necessary, provide her with financial and healthcare assistance.*

I am a US citizen and would be grateful if the US Consulate acted favorably and promptly on Ms. Krupičková's request for a US visa.

Sincerely,
Simon Reznikov

He released the guide and rotated the platen knob clockwise until most of the sheet was out of the typewriter's grip. He then proofread the invitation, rotated the knob in the opposite direction and typed the letter 'r' over the word "Czechoslovakia," crossing it out as well as he could. He rotated the knob just a touch and typed "the Czech Republic" above the blacked-out name of the country which the land of his birth caressed with tanks and jackboots in 1968, just as he was learning to walk in the streets of Moscow. He smiled like a blind jazz pianist, rolled the page off the platen, folded it, and placed it in an airmail envelope. It was the only envelope he had in his room, and he wrote "Milena

Krupičková, Prague" on it, thinking of the lonesome boy in Chekhov's story, who inscribed the envelope with the tremulous words "to grandpa's at the village."

Taking some money from a stash he kept in his toiletry kit, Simon headed down to the tram stop. He bought a bunch of waxy tulips from a flower girl. Should I just ask Milena to marry me right here on the spot? Simon thought, as he walked past the interchangeable hippies strumming their guitars on the bridge. Just take my grandmother's old ring off my pinkie and give it to her? he reasoned with an imaginary double who was called Syoma. For some reason Simon was convinced that Milena would say "yes." But his Russian double, was he also sure?

When Simon and Milena came out of the bar, holding glasses of white wine, Simon noticed Frantík, Milena's ex-boyfriend, watching them from a bookshop across the street. By the time they had found two empty chairs on the sidewalk and pulled them together, the jealous musician was gone.

Silently they sipped their wine, the rims of their hands joining and coming apart like blades of grass in the wind.

Breaking the silence, Simon asked, "Milena, I wanted to ask you something."

"Ask me," Milena said, lowering her angled chin onto her left shoulder.

"Would you like to come and stay with me this summer?"

"In America?"

"Yes, in America. In New Haven, to be precise. But first you would fly to New York."

"The Kennedy Airport, like in spy novels?" Milena asked.

"Exactly. And then we'll drive to New Haven, and I'll take you around and show you New England. We can visit my folks in Boston. See Cape Cod and the ocean. There's lots to do."

"Will you have time for me?"

Simon hesitated, then reached for his breast pocket and removed the airmail envelope he had prepared for her.

"I didn't have another kind," he said.

"This is for me?" Milena asked.

"I've typed up an invitation. You'll need to take it to the American embassy in Prague. Here, open it."

Milena slowly read the invitation, her lips mouthing some of the words. She blushed, then composed herself and said, trying to find the right English words,

"Simon, you surprised me. May I please think about it?"

They crossed to the other side, holding hands. The Vltava, swollen with the spring torrents, carried urban detritus under the arches of the bridge. There are sixteen of them, Simon remembered Milena telling him the first time they walked together across the Charles Bridge. Yelping and thrashing, a Maltese was trying to rip its leash from the hands of its owner, an old lady wearing a mauve hat with flowers. Small dogs, big tempers, Simon wanted to quote one of his father's aphorisms but hesitated. He thought of his parents in Boston, of the daily Russian phone calls, and he felt a double pang of sadness, which Russian immigrants sometimes feel when traveling in Europe.

At the circle near Malostranské Square, he offered to walk Milena to her car.

"I'm meeting my girlfriend Agáta. I'll drop her off and then drive home," Milena said, a bit vaguely.

"Are you sure?" he asked, feebly.

"There's your tram, go. I'll pick you up at the house at ten in the morning."

"I love you, Milena," he yelled through the tram's closing doors.

She took him to the airport in her mother's car. At the check-in counter, an agent with heavy makeup and retainers on her teeth weighed Simon's suitcase and told him it was fifteen kilos over the limit. All the archival stuff, Simon thought, hundreds of pages. Plus the souvenirs. And the two painted plates he bought from Milena's friend Katka, each of them wrapped, like mummies, in layers and layers of newsprint. But it still felt like extortion, and he asked to speak with the supervisor.

A pasty-faced man came out of some back door and handed Simon a card with the words "J. Biskup. Engineer. Czech Airlines."

"My luggage is under the piece concept, not based on weight," Simon said, stringing together some strange English words he had only heard but never used before.

"Yes, you're correct, from Paris to New York, but from Prague to Paris it is on the weight basis."

"This is a rip-off," Simon said. "I want to see a Delta representative. I booked through Delta, not Czech Airlines."

"I'm a Delta representative," Engineer Biskup replied. "And I'm making you a special offer. Fifty dollars for the extra weight. Or perhaps you would prefer to leave the suitcase in the care of the young lady," he added, injecting venom into his smile.

Simon removed a credit card from of his well-worn amber wallet. "Soviet habits die hard," he said loudly, turning to Milena, who put an index finger to her lips.

The agent with retainers on her teeth tagged his suitcase and handed him the boarding pass. "Checked all the way to New York."

Simon and Milena walked in the direction of passport control.

"Let we say a goodbye like the good friends," Milena said, suddenly losing a grip on her English grammar.

Simon didn't understand why she was trying to phrase it this way.

"I have a present for you." Milena reached for her satchel and took out a parcel wrapped in silver gift paper.

They were standing right before the entrance to the passport control corridor. A female border guard shamelessly watched their parting.

"I want you to open it on the plane. Do you promise?"

"Why? Yes, I promise."

"You should go now, you'll miss your flight."

"When will you go to the embassy?" he asked.

"Next week, I just need to talk this over with my parents."

He picked up his carry-on bag and walked toward the passport control kiosks.

"I'll call you from New Haven," he shouted, turning around to Milena, who waved, looking past him.

A morose lieutenant at passport control brought back more memories of leaving Moscow for good.

"Are you still a citizen of the Russian Federation?" the Czech lieutenant asked.

"No, why?" Simon asked.

"It says in your passport that you were born in Russia," the lieutenant replied, barely lifting his head from Simon's passport.

"I'm a US citizen," Simon answered, trying to hide his welling irritation. Then he added, more calmly, "They took away our Soviet citizenship in 1987 when we left."

The Czech lieutenant stamped his passport and nudged it toward Simon. Simon turned to wave to Milena one last time, but she was already gone.

Waiting at the gate, Simon was tempted to open the present but held back. Then they announced boarding.

A mustached burly man sitting next to him on the plane turned out to be an American from Texas, who had just spent almost a month investigating his ancestors' Moravian roots. Upon hearing that Simon was a doctoral student from a famous university, the Moravian from Texas tried his homegrown, drawled Czech dialect on Simon, then took out copies of various community records and old photographs to show him; and by the time their Soviet-made jet had started skewering puffy clouds, Simon's fellow traveler was already initiating Simon into the history of Moravian settlements in Texas and inviting him to his hometown of Ennis to attend the annual Czech Heritage Day and polka festival. The drinks service rescued Simon from the clutches of the Texan, who had to put away his bag to make room for the tray.

"Do you like our Becherovka?" the Texan asked, beaming with pride.

"I'm not sure," Simon replied.

"Give him a Becherovka," the Texan said to the flight attendant. "If you don't like it, I'll drink it," the Texan said, turning to Simon, and exploded with laughter.

Simon quietly asked for a glass of mineral water.

"Good stuff," the Texan commented. "Comes from under the mountain of Bořeň."

Simon closed his eyes and didn't answer. A few minutes later he glanced at his gregarious neighbor out of the corner of his right eye. The Texan had downed his Becherovka and was leaning back in his seat, mouth half open, eyelids drooping down. Simon waited a few more minutes for his neighbor to doze off, then reached for his carry-on and felt for Milena's present with the tips of his fingers. Trying not to spill his drinks, he slid the parcel out of his bag, placed it on his knees, and slowly tore off the wrapping.

It was a volume of Gregor's stories, translated into Czech, and published in Brno in 1929. Simon touched the greenish binding, then gently opened the volume to the title page. Inside, attached with a small plastic clip, was a note in Milena's Gothic scrawl. Simon quickly read the note, put it back in the book, and downed his Becherovka. Then he reclined in his seat and sat, eyes shut, trying to force his mind to annihilate the past month. Would that the whole trip to Prague were a dream, Simon thought. A long dream one could write down in one's journal and then turn the page. Again his hand reached for the Gregor volume, removed Milena's letter and brought it to his eyes:

Lásko,

I cannot do this.

You could be the best man I'll ever meet. But I don't know it. And I'm afraid of testing destiny.

I love my country and my family. I cannot imagine living away from home. And I know that you have already left a home once in your life. And you love your America.

The past few weeks have been happiness, and I thank you for it.

Please I beg you don't call me or write me. There is no future in this.

When your book about Felix Gregor comes out, please send me a copy to the
library. They will get in touch with me.
With much sadness in my heart,
Milena K.

Simon Reznikov used to relish the sensation of returning home from abroad.
Having once lived for six years as a stateless person, he loved to think of
America as his country. It used to be so exciting to go through US border
control. "Hello, officer," Simon would say almost brashly, hiding traces of his
Russian accent. "Welcome back," the officer would reply after stamping his
passport, and this stamping and crossing gave Simon's eternal refugee a sense
of belonging. He was anchored to this place, his home was here in America,
everything was going to be okay . . .

Before getting his suitcase and diving into JFK's many-tongued,
overheated crowd, Simon called his parents from a pay phone.

"*Eto ya.* Alive and well. Yes, very good flight. You're both healthy? Love
you, call you when I get home."

After a frazzling cab ride to Grand Central, he was on a Metro-North train
bound for New Haven. During the almost two-hour train trip he had trouble
focusing on anything. The euphoria of arrival, that squirrel of an emotion, had
turned into a different creature—a mule of indecision. Simon looked out the
window at the bobbing shoreline of Connecticut, the bridges, the gas stations
and truck stops, the tire plants and sausage factories. He talked for a while to
a lady from the Bronx going to see her sister and nephews in Stratford. Then
he pressed his head to the dusty window. Salt marshes, rust-colored and flung
open to sun and wind, brought to mind the armpits of a giant female bather.
Indifferent objects and associations—the floral skirt of a girl sitting across
the aisle or a red Audi parked at a commuter station—returned Milena to his
thoughts.

He got home around eight in the evening to discover that his apartment
had been burglarized. They had only taken his stereo and leather jacket—the
thieves hadn't even checked the closet where Simon hid his trusty old Mac

behind shoeboxes and storage bins. Simon accepted the break-in as some sort of a payment levied upon him by fate. He knocked on the door of his downstairs neighbor, a medical resident with red cheeks and dewy skin who was also an ordained minister and played bass. Simon's nickname for the neighbor was "Albert Schweitzer." The neighbor had been doing a rotation at Waterbury Hospital and hadn't heard anything.

"You lose you gain," he said and offered Simon a beer.

Simon didn't even call the police.

The next morning, after unpacking and a long phone call with his parents, Simon went out to get groceries. He liked to go to a little neighborhood store run by an older Italian couple. After grocery shopping and combined breakfast and lunch with strong black tea, Simon went out again to get his mail, which was being held at the local post office, and also to drop off a few shirts. It was the second week of May. Summer school, where Simon was to teach Russian, wasn't starting for three more weeks. He would have some time to sort through all the material he had brought back from Prague, get some dissertation work done, and possibly even start talking to publishers about "The Jew's Castle" with his introduction and commentary.

Walking back with a plastic tote full of mail, Simon took in the smells of New England's blossoms, his eyes gliding along Victorian turrets and treetops. At the corner, near the entrance to a laundromat, Simon saw Money-Change. One of the regulars, this man of about fifty would stand for hours at the corner, a stogie glued to his rectangular lower lip, and mumble the same phrase: "money-change, money-change, money-change."

Money-Change accosted Simon as he would anyone who passed buy, and he reached to fish a quarter out of his jeans pocket. And it was then Simon suddenly thought to himself: Look, here I am, the world around seems perfectly normal, except that only yesterday morning I was driving with Milena to the airport through the streets of Prague . . .

Simon walked back to the apartment and dialed Milena's number.

"*Ano*," her father answered.

Simon panicked and dropped the receiver.

A restlessness gripped him. He strode across the grounds of the nearby Theological Seminary, then came home and tried to take a nap. "I need to clear my head," Simon said to himself. He ran down to the basement, where the landlord let him keep his bike and fishing gear in a recess in the wall beside the boiler. Simon had been a fisherman his whole life, having learned the skill from his father during their annual summer trips to Estonia. In New England, with its wide open beaches and stocked lakes and ponds, both freshwater and saltwater fishing had been raised to a new level.

Simon drove to East Haven, stopping at a bait and tackle store on the way to Lighthouse Park. He usually fished from the same spot, where at high tide flounder liked to congregate between pylons under the shadow of the deck. As he approached the pier, he saw a short heavyset man in rough canvas pants, a gray Yale hoodie and a black, knitted cap, who was fishing from his spot. The man had two rods, each propped up against the top rail. Simon grimly walked up to the intruder and glanced in his green bucket. There were four flatfish with oval-shaped, speckled bodies in the bucket. Lucky dog, Simon thought, studying the fisherman's face—brows black and bushy, eyes moist and acorn-hued, lips full and protruded. The man standing at Simon's spot smiled, revealing uneven teeth, and Simon put down his white, scratched bucket next to that of the stranger, and started to assemble his folded rod.

"Nice going," Simon said, nodding toward the man's bucket.

"Thanks," the man replied, a smile still hovering over his face.

"Whatcha using for bait?" Simon asked, a bit obnoxiously, lifting from the bucket his backpack with tackle.

"I use worm," the man said, a Hispanic accent now clearly audible in his English. He reached for a plastic container at his feet, picked it up and shook its contents before Simon's face. Simon saw fat pearly worms stirring in grainy dirt.

"You're using earth worms as bait for flounder?" Simon asked.

"She love it," the fisherman said.

Careful not to be stung, Simon took a bronze sandworm from a cardboard box lined with seaweed. He hooked the sandworm through its mouth and dropped the line straight under the pier. When the sinker hit the bottom, Simon gathered the slack, leaned his rod on the railing and turned to his chance fishing companion. Now relaxed, he introduced himself, and the fisherman, who was from Guatemala, didn't even suspect that Simon was also an immigrant. They struck up a conversation.

The Guatemalan used to be a coffee grower back home. He had come to America six years ago and worked as a custodian at "the university," mainly doing the evening shift. He spoke with pride about his job and his three children, who were scholarship students at St. Bernadette School. Two immigrants fishing for flounder, Simon thought, as he reeled in and checked his rig, taking off a half-bitten worm, oozing blood where the point of the wide-gap hook had come out. He replaced it with a fresh one, dropped the line again and waited, watching the tip of his rod. The Guatemalan fisherman pulled out one more flounder, measured it, and nodded with contentment before placing it in his bucket. He folded his rods and fastened the top halves to the bottom halves with heavy rubber bands.

"Take it," he said to Simon, offering his container with soil and worms. "She love it!"

"I'll stick to sandworms. Thank you."

Simon checked his rig again and replaced a tattered worm with a fresh one. He shot a glance in the direction of the parking lot, where the Guatemalan man was getting into a crimson wagon. Then the tip of Simon's rod came alive with a thump. Slowly bringing in the slack, Simon counted to eleven, set the hook with a measured jerking motion, and began to reel in the fish, feeling with his whole body the zigzagging path of the flounder's resistance. He pulled the flounder's flopping, oblong body over the rail, laid it on the boards and measured it.

"Two inches over the keeper size," Simon murmured, admiring his flounder and calling it by its dactylic Russian name, *kambala*, which he associated with something songlike, lilting.

The flounder's silvery fins framed its perfectly shaped form. A pale blue line divided its greenish back with brown and maroon speckles in two elliptical halves. In striking contrast to the symmetry of the flounder's body, both of its eyes were bulging off-center, as if they had trouble seeing the world in its fullness. Simon peered into the flounder's skyward eyes, and he saw his own immigrant longing reflected on their greenish surface.

Holding the flounder's body with both hands, like a freshly varnished mandolin, Simon placed it in the bucket. He took a deep breath, baited the hook and dropped the line.

BROTHERLY LOVE

From his Soviet youth Simon Reznikov missed camaraderie the most. He had been in America for nearly nine years, and yet his best male friends were still living in the old country. He had made new friends in college and graduate school, but it just wasn't the same. In Russia they were like brothers to one another. They cared about each other no less passionately than they did about the girls they loved. How they admired one another' youthful wit and abandon. It was nearly impossible to explain to an American. This male friendship, this bond.... Brotherly love! They showed affection for each other through hugging and patting, even kissing. It would never occur to them, back in the days of Soviet innocence and puritanism, that bodily contacts were anything but expressions of brotherly love. After living in America for some time, Simon the immigrant had begun to cultivate an image of himself and his old Soviet friends as something of a cross between Arthurian knights and lion cubs.

All this had everything and nothing to do with an e-mail Simon received in April 1996. He had just defended his dissertation and was waiting to hear from the colleges he had interviewed with about teaching jobs. The email came on a Friday morning, April 12th, the old Soviet Day of Cosmonautics. It displayed an economy of words: "I've moved to Conn., a systems admin. job. The rest when I see you. AM."

The initials "AM" stood for Aleksandra Mironova, or "Sashenka," as everybody called her back in Moscow.

Simon telephoned Sashenka on the evening of the Day of Cosmonautics. Two days later, on a sunny Saturday morning, he drove from New Haven to see her. Route 91 was empty all the way to the outskirts of Hartford. Twice, Simon listened to "Because You Loved Me" by Celine Dion on different stations, singing along and keeping rhythm with his left hand. When he wasn't singing along or reading the rural landscape, he let his memory ebb and flow. Fate itself was taking him to a rendezvous with the past . . .

Simon had met Sashenka in the summer of 1986. He was nineteen, a rising third-year university student majoring in philology, and had just returned from a seven-week research trip to the deep south of Russia. During this folklore-collecting expedition, a group of them traveled in a ramshackle bus from one Russian village to another, recording old people's stories and songs. They slept in tents and cooked their own meals. There were fifteen in the group, including two faculty members, a married graduate student and a driver, so there was little chance of romance. And they never stayed in any given place for more than two or three nights, which didn't leave much time to court the local collective farm belles. By the end of the trip Simon had grown his first beard, curlier and lighter than his hair. His skin felt like the outside of an old sheepskin coat: layers of dust, salt, and sun.

Simon returned to Moscow at the end of July. After collecting his pay for the expedition work, which came to almost 120 rubles, three times the monthly stipend he received at the university, Simon felt rich and grown-up. A few days later he and his parents took a night express train for Estonia. Like most of his friends in Moscow, Simon was still living at home with parents, and Estonia had for many years been the annual destination of their summer escape. That summer, between his second and third university years, Simon for the first time didn't share a seaside apartment with his mother and father, but roomed with three of his best friends who had rented a cottage and were already in Estonia waiting for him to join them.

The name of the blessed Estonian resort where Simon had spent a total of three years—adding up all the summers he had been there first as a kid, then as a teenager and university student—was Pärnu. This Baltic resort stood on the west coast of Estonia, about a two-hour drive from Estonia's capital, Tallinn. Pärnu enjoyed a heyday during Estonia's brief spell of independence. Then came the Soviet annexation in 1940, then the Nazi occupation, and finally the Soviet "liberation," which lasted for almost fifty years. During the Soviet era the waterfront Rannahotel, a landmark of Estonian functionalism, was turned into a vacation home for Communist Party officials, heroic miners, and valiant cotton growers. Many streets were given Soviet names, but the town retained much of its prewar character, as even years of Soviet rule couldn't take the Northern European breeding out of the local population, nor could it remove the Gothic roofs from the local Soviet offices.

When Simon and his parents first came to Pärnu in 1970, they were enchanted by the Estonian lifestyle. There were still people everywhere who grew up during the country's prewar independence. Estonia felt strikingly foreign. Even before they attempted to emigrate, Simon's mother, a violinist in a chamber orchestra, and his father, a research biochemist and playwright, had been dreaming about traveling abroad. After they became refuseniks, Simon's father lost his research position; his name was blacklisted and his plays were no longer performed. His mother was fired from the orchestra. In their new life as outcasts, Simon's father became a foreman at a plastics factory, and his mother gave violin lessons at home. For ten years, as emigration remained their obsession, summers in Estonia gave them an annual foretaste of Europe and the West.

More than two thirds of the resort's summer population were Jewish professionals from big Soviet cities. Summer after summer, Russian-speaking Jewish kids who had known each other since early childhood would congregate on the beach and compete in ball games, or go to movies together. The core of Simon's Pärnu gang of friends was formed when they were seven or eight and played Cowboys and Indians under the tepid Baltic sun. Many of the parents were friendly, forming their own *kompaniya*, gathering at the same spot on the beach and having little soirées at night, where they told political jokes and consumed large quantities of the local Bénédictine. Both kids and parents dreaded the end of August . . .

On the train from Moscow to Tallinn, lying on the upper berth of the compartment he shared with his parents and a Jewish widow, Simon couldn't fall asleep, elated with anticipation of seeing his friends. Their names were Misha, short for Mikhail, Tima, a diminutive of Timofey, and Igor—just Igor for he didn't like diminutives.

Misha Tyshler was six feet one, bespectacled, skinny, and jittery. Proust and Musil were his literary idols, and Antonioni and Chabrol his favorite film directors. Misha had weak eyes but refused to wear stronger glasses. He couldn't see clearly, which sometimes made him an object of teasing. From a distance every girl with a pretty figure stirred up his imagination. Misha was studying TV production as he fantasized about directing films.

Tima Obnorsky would have been perfect for the part of the dreamy nobleman Ilya Oblomov, the title character of the classic Russian novel about inaction. The baby-faced Tima dressed in older men's comfortable trousers and wool cardigans. His maternal grandfather was a member of the Academy of Sciences, a physicist who helped build the Soviet hydrogen bomb. Tima's whole demeanor exhibited a blend of sluggishness and intelligence. In the Pärnu gang, Tima was something of an exception since no known Jewish blood flowed in his veins—not that there was no Jewish blood in the veins of the Russian nobility. Tima loved Jewish dishes such as chopped herring or stuffed carp, clandestinely collected Israeli music, and taught himself the Hebrew alphabet "just for kicks."

Igor Lastikov was the third friend and companion of Simon's last summer in Estonia, and also the last one to join their brotherhood. Igor added himself to the cohort when they were all university freshmen, and they had only known him for about two years. Igor was short and muscular, and a bluish Levantine shadow never left his cheeks and chin. Like most young Jews in the Soviet Union of the 1980s, he was doomed to pursue a degree in engineering. Igor knew the ways of the world, and the gang needed one street-smart fellow among its romantics. Many things about Igor appealed to Simon from the first moment he surfaced at one of Misha's Saturday parties. Igor's fearlessness came across as natural—not the lack of fear that Simon had trained himself to showcase after being taunted in second and third grade, but the instinct of a strong young animal. Even when his mouth laughed, Igor's dark eyes were alert.

Igor's family was also quite unusual. A manager at a construction company, his father spent his days at excavation pits cursing workers and going over blueprints with civil engineers. He was a heavy drinker and a great connoisseur of Russian swear words. Igor's mother stayed home and knitted sweaters and dresses, which she sold to private clients. They did quite well financially, but for some reason continued to live in a communal apartment they shared with four other families. It was in the heart of old Moscow, only a few blocks from the old stage of the Moscow Art Theater and the headquarters of the Moscow Criminal Police. They shared one huge room, and Igor slept at the far end behind a mahogany armoire. Igor's parents vacationed in Crimea and would not have meshed well with the crowd that surrounded Simon and his friends in Estonia . . .

Simon and his parents arrived in Tallinn from Moscow early in the morning and were in Pärnu by noon. The streets smelled of peat and of granite dust. The cottage Simon's friends had rented was about a fifteen-minute walk from the waterfront. The walls had settled so much that one could look inside the windows from the street. Tulle curtains fluttered in the breeze. Simon entered through a picket gate and saw a little garden with a couple of wooden chairs and an overfilled ashtray on a three-legged stool. Gooseberry shrubs grew in the middle of the yard, and a raspberry jungle covered the perimeter. Simon picked a few nipply raspberries and immediately burned his ankles on the nettles that guarded the raspberry bushes. He went inside though the unlocked back door. In the kitchen, Igor was holding court. Wearing only boxer shorts and a red apron, he was making a gargantuan omelet in a cast iron pan.

"Igor," Simon said in a low voice. "I'd like some omelet too."

"Syomka, you son of a gun," Igor screamed. He put down a spatula and jumped at Simon, hugging him and patting him on both shoulders. "Didn't even tell us you were coming today. You look real tough with that beard." He felt Simon's biceps.

"And Misha? Tima? Where are they?" Simon asked.

"Those losers would sleep until noon if I didn't wake them. They only get up when breakfast is ready."

Simon checked out the rest of the cottage. Besides the country kitchen with a wood stove, there were four iron beds, an old table covered with an oil cloth, and a small adjacent room cluttered with old furniture and toys. The outhouse toilet was an ancient affair with a cycloptic hole and the bowels of the earth brooding underneath. There was a faucet with running cold water in the kitchen but no shower or tub.

"What do you think?" Igor asked.

"Excellent," Simon said.

"Not too shabby for six rubles a day, huh?" Igor said. Then he ordered: "Go wake up those lazy bums."

Simon took the pan with the omelet that gave out a pungent smells of fried scallions and cheese, and went into the bedroom.

"*Zavtrak podan*," he sang out. "Breakfast's served. Time to get up, fellas."

Misha was the first to open his eyes. He groped on his nightstand for cigarettes. With his eyes closed he lay there for another minute, inhaling his morning smoke. Then he put on his spectacles and asked in a groggy, happy voice,

"Syomka, come free us from tyranny?"

Misha picked up a tattered book from his nightstand.

"Look what I found at a secondhand bookstore here," Misha said, handing Simon a turn-of-the-century Russian translation of Knut Hamsun's *Hunger*.

Simon went up to Tima's bed and pulled off the blanket. Tima slept in a long flannel nightshirt.

"Syoma," he said. "He makes us wash the dishes and go grocery shopping."

Igor barreled in on his short muscular legs and yelled, acting the part of a Russian drill sergeant: "Come on, slobs. The food's getting cold."

For breakfast, in addition to the thick omelet that looked like a soufflé, Igor served a salad of sliced tomatoes and cucumbers with a dill sour cream dressing, a loaf of Estonian *sepik* bread with caraway seeds, and slices of smoked cheese. A pot of coffee and a jug of milk stood on the table. The aroma of chicory rising up from the pot brought to Simon's tongue the familiar taste of Estonian summer.

"You can't possibly imagine how horny I am," said Simon, languorously.

"I can," said the phlegmatic Tima.

"I can't," said Misha proudly.

It turned out that Misha had been having a fling with Lyuba, whose nickname was "Otter," so as not to confuse her with another Lyuba they had known since childhood—Lyuba the "Globe."

"You need to find yourself a dame," Igor said to Simon.

"Just me? Don't you want to get laid?" Simon asked Igor.

Igor lit a cigarette and let out a long puff.

"Not as badly as you do."

"If you say so," Simon said. "Now, could someone tell me who's around?"

"Let Misha do it. He's our Proust," Tima said. Then he turned to Igor and added: "We need to get more of this red currant jam."

Misha got up and started pacing up and down the room. The floor squeaked melodiously to the rhythm of his pacing. "Let's see. Katya Kats is here. Yulya's here."

"Which Yulya?" Simon slipped in the question.

"Yulya the Doughnut, obviously. The other Yulya got married. Okay, who else? Oh, yes, Masha the violist and also Masha from Tashkent. Let's see, Katyusha Levina is supposedly coming next week. Oh, I know who else is around. Saba is here with two girlfriends. They're staying in the mustard house at the corner, where there's a bakery and a liquor store."

"I know the place," Simon said. "Tolya used to rent it." Tolya Shapiro, one of the original kids in their Pärnu gang, had emigrated to Israel in 1979.

"Who are the girlfriends?" Simon asked.

"I bumped into them yesterday near the tennis courts," Misha replied. "Veronika—we met her at Saba's. The other's new."

Of course, they didn't make it to the beach until the afternoon, and there were no chairs left at the rental place, and the beer at the seaside kiosk still tasted the same—of Estonian country bread and salt water. Wading slowly into the Baltic shallows, Simon felt again the joy of returning to a place where he had come to know himself, where many sunbathers remembered him as a child, and where memories rolled in his head like sand across dunes.

In the evening, after a long nap and a dinner of fried yellow perch, macaroni with butter and grated cheese, lettuce salad, and cheap Algerian red wine, the four of them headed in the direction of the waterfront. At night young people's social activities moved to badminton and tennis courts at the center of a seaside park. Rows of green wooden benches encircled the courts, and on these benches the gang would sit for hours, trading witticisms. Sometimes a couple would vanish into one of the dark alleys covered with red gravel. On the edge of the park, close to the town's fanciest quarter, there was an old amusement park with a Ferris wheel and the art nouveau building of the former casino. Just as the country had felt the first pangs of reforms in the mid-1980s, a cocktails lounge opened in the former casino. There was a sickening dearth of entertainment for Soviet young people, and Simon would later tell American acquaintances how they fantasized about sitting in a smoky jazz bar somewhere in New York City or in an open air café in Nice. Just sitting there for hours on end, sipping cocktails, smoking, and people watching.

Lyuba the Otter, Misha's love interest that summer, met them outside the new cocktail lounge. There were half a dozen people in line ahead of them, all of them Estonians. The Estonian youths got in very quickly as Simon and his friends braced up for a long wait. It had happened to them before that an Estonian manager would make Russian-speaking clients stand outside a bar or restaurant even though there were free tables. After forty minutes of waiting, Igor was getting ready to bang on the door when it opened, and the hostess escorted them to a table in a dimly lit corner of the lounge.

"Look, Saba and her girlfriends are here," Misha said.

Chairs were added to the table, and two minutes later they were gossiping about a certain very fashionable Moscow actor who had been seen in town riding in a red Volkswagen, a rare bug among Soviet insects on wheels. Saba was a tall, lively redhead, a student of French and Spanish at the Moscow Pedagogical University. Her father had designed several government buildings in Moscow before dying of a heart attack when Saba was seven or eight. Saba wrote self-denuding love poems à la Tsvetaeva and hosted dance parties in her spacious Moscow apartment off Gorky Street. Deep inside, Simon resented Saba a bit because of the set she belonged to—those official Jews who, unlike his own parents, behaved as though they were winning at the Soviet game. But did these things matter on a summer vacation? Did he think of it as his gaze passed across the face of one of Saba's girlfriends and then halted? This is how Simon remembered Sashenka when he first met her in Pärnu: brown eyes and ashen locks down to her shoulders. A slightly upturned nose. Dimpled cheeks. Sashenka's white, sleeveless blouse went perfectly with the shades of her face and the smoky darkness. If there's such a thing as Soviet picture-perfect, Sashenka lived as a picture-perfect girl in Simon's memories of his last Soviet summer.

The next evening Simon swung by the mustard house with a mansard roof, where Sashenka and her girlfriends rented two connecting rooms. Simon and Sashenka walked, hand in hand, to the far side of the beach in the direction of the stone jetties. It had rained in the afternoon and, as they strolled through the park, the evening sun licked the moisture off alleys and benches. Sashenka told him that before her parents got divorced, they used to go to Berdyansk on the Sea of Azov. In middle and high school she would spend two months at a summer camp outside Moscow. Ah, young pioneer camps, Simon was thinking to himself as he listened to Sashenka. Soviet unsentimental education. . . . Sashenka was wearing white tennis shoes, a lemon sleeveless shirt with buttons on the back, and tan shorts. She told Simon she made most of her clothes, getting the ideas from the Polish *Uroda* and other Eastern Bloc fashion magazines. From the corner of his eye Simon kept looking at Sashenka's slender ankles.

There were two stone jetties that ran parallel to each other, stretching for over a mile from the estuary of the Pärnu River into gulf. One started at the very end of the beach, past the ladies' nude section, where as teenagers they would venture, binoculars around their necks, and hide behind the dunes. Growing up, Simon used to go fishing off the jetty with his father, and they would bring home bagfuls of perch, roach and tench, as well as the occasional eel and flounder. Both jetties were constructed in the 1860s out of granite boulders, abundant in those parts where the glacier had once wreaked havoc. Sashenka and Simon walked to the very end of the jetty, where a veteran lighthouse blinked time with a red, watery eye, and where only flattened cans of beer and ripped fishing gear reminded one of the life panting at the shore.

Driving from New Haven to a rendezvous with his Soviet past, Simon remembered the jetty and the lighthouse, and the silky tremor of Sashenka's fingers enmeshed in his. And he also remembered kissing Sashenka on the jetty's last, bulbous boulder. Briny kissing, waves lashing at the jetty. The youthful rapture of wanting and being wanted. And across the bay—the drunken lights of the Ferris wheel.

If this were an American story of summertime romance, Sashenka's American version and Simon's own double might have gone to a motel or made love on the back seat of an old Chevy Malibu Classic. But this was a Soviet tale, and like most Soviet *innamorati*, Sashenka and Simon didn't have a place where they could be alone. The rooms she was sharing with two other girlfriends or Simon's own "barracks" were out of the question. Simon's tolerant parents came to his rescue two or three days later. The plan was for his parents to go out after supper and not come back for a couple of hours; and they agreed that Simon would leave his key in the lock so as to indicate that he and Sashenka were still there. Dressed in his father's terry robe, Simon paced up and down the apartment. After almost an hour of waiting, Simon gave up, thinking angrily that Sashenka had changed her mind. He moved over to the kitchen window and lit one of his mother's menthol cigarettes. His eyes followed the flight of obese seagulls. He smoked, trying to convince himself that it was only a partial disaster, and that his lover's luck hadn't run out. Then the buzzer finally rang. Simon dashed to the door.

"What happened?"

Sashenka was flushed, out of breath.

"Please don't be mad. Saba and Veronika were supposed to return at six, and they were late, and we only have one key. I'm really sorry."

He led her into the room. His parents' bed stood in an alcove. There was also a low divan by the window, and Simon and Sashenka sat on it. Simon looked at his watch before taking it off. His fingers found a plastic hook on the front of Sashenka's bra, and then circled about her waist before locating a zipper on the side of her linen pants. Then a key was inserted into the door and turned half way. Sashenka clenched Simon's shoulders and looked up at him with terror. The key was turned back and yanked out of the lock. There was vexed coughing outside the apartment door, and then the sound of feet marching in place. And then, drowning in the stairwell, the staccato of woman's heels and the thumping of man's soles.

"It's okay," Simon said. "My parents know the code. I left a key in the door, which means we're still here."

"God, Syoma, I was scared."

After making love, they sat in the kitchen, wearing his parents' robes and drinking tea with lemon.

Later that evening, when they got to the beach, the tide was low, and the water perfectly still. Like ice skaters, dunlins glided up and down the ribbed sandbar. The ripe August sun hauled its tired body over the charcoal horizon. It was the end of a long day of playing by the sea, and sunset swimming was a favorite pastime in Pärnu. Near the cracked parapet they ran into Misha and Lyuba, Tima, Igor, and a few other young people who were preparing to go into the water.

"Syomochka and Sashenka," Igor greeted them. "Well, well. Did you two have a good time?"

He patted Simon on the back, winking at him and grinning. There was nothing unusual in Igor's conduct. Friendly bantering was part of brotherly love. His friends, Misha and Tima, didn't think for a minute that there might be something strange in Igor's comment.

Igor put himself in charge of the group's evening frolic.

"Okay, people, listen up," he said in his commanding voice. "Girls to the left, boys to the right, men and women straight ahead."

After the swim, followed by coffee at a café with glass walls painted with mermaids, Saba invited the whole group over to play charades. While they walked up Karuselli Street—Pärnu's longest thoroughfare—Igor pulled

Simon by the sleeve. Sashenka and Simon unclasped their hands, and Simon and Igor fell behind the procession.

"You seem upset," Simon said as he put his arm around Igor's back.

Igor shook off his hand.

"What's the matter with you?" he said. "Are you blind? The blow-job princess has you twisted around her finger."

"What are you talking about?"

"What I'm talking about?" Igor blurted out. "Did you lose your wits out in the buttfuck south? The next thing you know, she'll get herself pregnant and you'll have to marry her. I know you—you wouldn't leave a poor shiksa in distress."

"A poor shiksa?" Simon repeated, bewildered for his friend. "Since when are you such a Jewish nationalist?"

"Since always," Igor replied. "I know how it works. The Russian broad comes to Pärnu in search of a nice Jewish boy. And please don't tell me you're in love."

"Not in love, but I could be. Listen, Igor, why does Sashenka bother you so much?"

"You don't understand," Igor forced out through his smallish porcelain teeth. "You come from a different world. Co-op apartment, nice neighborhood, good school. But I grew up with these people. Half of my neighbors have daughters like that."

"Let it go, Igor," Simon said. "Be happy for me."

"I'm not," said Igor and spat on a cobblestone.

Sashenka was walking ahead of them with Saba and Veronika. It had been such a perfect day that Igor's sudden outburst didn't upset Simon's serenity. At least, he didn't make much of it at the time. Igor never mentioned Sashenka again for the rest of their vacation. He was never hostile towards her, but he quietly ignored her. Then one day he showed up at the beach with a petite young woman with dark frizzy hair. Her name was Polina, and she was studying cello at the Leningrad Conservatory of Music. She was a smoker and swore with artistry; her red bikini was the skimpiest among the girls in their circle. Polina was renting her own room a couple of blocks from the town's old market near the public baths, and Igor began to stay over there. Tima and Misha breathed with relief after he had relinquished his duties as their vacation paterfamilias.

A week before the end of August they organized a picnic in honor of Misha's twentieth birthday. Sashenka volunteered to cook, and Simon helped her do the shopping. They went to the farmers' market and bought a whole assortment of local summer vegetables and fruit: faceted tomatoes that looked like aging wrestlers; bumpy cukes that were bittersweet and crunchy; bunches of radishes, scallions, dill, and coriander; and strawberries and raspberries for dessert. Local apples gave off the aroma of vinegar. They bought two loafs of grey country bread and three pounds of hot-smoked herring, an Estonian delicacy. Sashenka baked a rhubarb pie the night before—another staple of Baltic summertime.

They took a bus to the village of Raeküla about five miles outside Pärnu. Some of their friends had already left. It was a smaller group this time: Misha and Lyuba; Igor and Polina; Tima; Saba (whom everybody was trying to pressure into seducing Tima); and Sashenka and Simon. They walked across a pine forest towards a secluded sandy beach on the high river bank. When Simon was eight or nine, he and his father discovered that beach while searching for a quiet fishing spot. No vacationers ever came there. Only an occasional Estonian boy with a fishing rod or a couple of local farmers in black beat-up hats, pushing their prewar bicycles, would step out of the forest onto the squeaky white sand.

After lazy games of volleyball, and a feast under an old willow with silverish leaves, the couples disappeared into the woods, leaving Tima to snooze in the shade and Saba to bake her gold-freckled body in what was left of the day's sun. Sashenka and Simon took a grassy path along the edge of the woods. Picking boysenberries, they walked until they came to a clearing, one side of which overlooked the river. They helped each other out of their bathing costumes and lay down on the ground strewn with fresh pine needles.

Kissing Sashenka's berry-tasting mouth, Simon looked over her shoulder onto the river. A fisherman in a wooden boat was reeling in a pike. The pike was giving him a fight, and when he was hauling it overboard, its upright body glimmered with a promise of pain. Simon pulled up on his elbows and looked at Sashenka, who arched her neck to kiss him.

When they got up, Sashenka's back was covered with an ornament of pine needles. Back at the beach, Timofey was asleep, snoring like a baby calf; Saba was reading an American paperback novel, its cover neatly wrapped in a newspaper. The others were in the water, which tasted on the lips like tea out of an earthen mug. After swimming and splashing, guys on girls, they sat in the warm shallow water until the sun started going down and a cool wind blew in from the sea.

A lizardy bus brought them back to the center of Pärnu, and they stood there for a while, listening to disco music coming from behind the wall of the old town fortress. It had suddenly dawned on them that it was already the third week of August, and in a week's time they were going to leave Estonia and return to Moscow and Leningrad, their universities, the mud-splattering Russian autumn.

Years later Simon would remember his last summer in Estonia as "farewell sex." As the last week of his Pärnu vacation was coming to a close, he thought more and more about his city routine in Moscow, and Sashenka receded into the past—a morocco leather album of memories, placed in a nightstand drawer and opened on a frosty December night.

For their last rendezvous at his parents' apartment, Sashenka came dressed in a black turtleneck and plaid skirt, her clothes underscoring the imminence of autumn.

"I can't, Syoma," she said, stopping his hands and giving him a butterfly kiss. "Not today."

"What's wrong?" Simon asked, trying to guess which of the two answers it would be.

"I'm afraid of losing you."

"You can't lose me," Simon said. "Those who meet here in Pärnu are bound to each other for life. Look at Misha and Tima and me. It's a brotherhood."

"But I'm not a brother. I'm just some girl you met on vacation."

"Sashenka, please let's not torment each other," he said. "What's the use?"

"Am I even going to see you in Moscow?" she asked on the verge of tears.

He pulled her into his lap and slid his hands under her turtleneck.

"Sashenka," he said. "I'm terribly fond of you, I think you know that. But my life in Moscow is very different from what you have seen here . . ."

Her eyes became wet and she looked away. Simon placed his right hand on the nape of her neck and pressed her head to his shoulder.

"Of course I'll call you. And we'll always be friends. Do you hear me?"

"Yes," she said, smiling a rickety smile.

Simon went to the kitchen and boiled water for tea, which they drank with red currant tarts, and Sashenka wasn't even embarrassed when they ran into his parents in the stairwell.

He walked her home. She was leaving the following morning with Saba and Veronika, and they planned to spend a couple of days in Tallinn, just hanging out and shopping for clothes. When Simon and Sashenka came to the mustard house with a weathercock atop its mossy roof, he pulled an envelope out of his jacket.

"So you wouldn't think that I don't care," Simon said, handing it to her .

He kissed her on the lips and walked towards the beach without looking back.

In the envelope was a poem Simon had composed for Sashenka. He was writing steadily at the time, and he usually copied new poems into a pocket notebook with a picture of a firebird on its cover. This lacquered notebook traveled with him from Moscow, to Vienna and Rome, and later to America; and Simon kept it on a bookshelf above his desk. But for some reason the poem he wrote for Sashenka didn't make it to the notebook, and Simon only remembered the opening lines: *Green blinds fell down,/ little heels cascaded down the stairs,/ you left and when saying goodbye/ injected me with loneliness.*

When Simon called Sashenka the day after he and his parents returned to Moscow, he heard disbelief in her voice. On a late August afternoon when Moscow's streets smelled of spoiled watermelons, Sashenka visited Simon at his apartment near the Ostankino TV tower. She looked so different in city clothes: a navy raincoat; black pumps; a silk blouse with a crimson cherry-red scarf; a black skirt. Her hair was pinned up and smelled of Mystère Rochas— a perfume that the French trade envoys decided to dump upon Soviet women.

His parents were out at a refusenik gathering. Simon showed her around the apartment and made Turkish coffee on the gas stove. For some reason Simon remembered that they talked about her father who was building a dacha south of Moscow. Sashenka was living in a one-bedroom with her mother and grandmother, a church-going peasant from a village in the Kaluga Province. Her parents were barely on speaking terms.

A worm of uncertainty was burrowing its way into Simon's head. He wanted to make love to Sashenka, but he also didn't want to say things he didn't believe, either before or after the lovemaking. Sashenka took off her skirt and Simon saw that instead of tights she had on a pair of stockings, strapped on to a black garter belt. Back in the Soviet Union of his youth, good nylon tights were hard to come by, and garter belts with stockings were something obsolete, old-fashioned, worn by middle-aged women hauling mesh bags full of groceries. Sashenka unstrapped and rolled off her stockings and took off the garter belt.

"I've managed to rip all my tights," she said with a guilty smile.

Simon didn't call her for a week after her visit, and he didn't return her phone calls.

Then came the most burlesque part of the story. Igor's birthday was on September 2—a fabulous time for a party. Everyone was back in town from summer trips; university classes just started; farmers' markets abounded with autumnal wares. Simon went to Igor's in the brightest of moods. Misha, Tima, and he met up in front of the Pushkin monument and walked together. They entered the cavernous communal apartment and passed through a faintly lit corridor. Much of the room was occupied by a long table heavy with dishes and bottles. Stocky jade bottles of Soviet black label champagne neighbored bottles of vodka and Georgian semisweet wine. At the center of the table there was a majolica dish with *satsivi*—Georgian-style chicken in walnut-garlic sauce. There was also salmon roe and smoked sturgeon, Hungarian salami, and ham from Yugoslavia, as well as all sorts of salads, garlicky and spicy spreads, and bunches of greens.

Savoring the thought of having a shot of cold vodka with salmon roe served inside a halved hard-boiled egg, Simon walked to the back of the room. He was saying hello to a couple of Igor's high school friends—she a student of ballet, he a future architect—when he saw Sashenka. She got up and stepped towards him from Igor's sofa, where she had been sitting with other guests. Sashenka—at Igor's birthday?

"Hi, Syoma," she said and kissed him on the cheek.

"Sashenka . . . what are you doing here?" he asked.

"I came to wish Igor a happy birthday."

Simon turned around and went to talk to Igor, who was fussing about the table, making sure there were enough plates and chairs for everyone.

"What are you doing?" Simon whispered.

"What do you mean, 'What am I doing?'"

"Why is she here?"

"I just thought you'd be glad to see her."

"This is ridiculous. Why didn't you tell me she was coming?"

"I thought it would make a nice surprise for you."

"Some surprise. First you call her a shiksa and a slut, then you invite her to your birthday."

There were moments when Simon's stomach turned into an acid waterfall. He would sit and concentrate his anger until it reached boiling point, which was when he needed to do something crazy, pull a prank, make a conquest. At the table, Simon ended up sitting next to Igor's college classmate by the name of Vadim. His nickname was Frog—not because he had French blood, but because of his voice. After they had a few drinks to toast Igor's health, Frog and Simon got up from the table and said they were going out for a smoke. They headed back to Pushkin Square and parked themselves on a bench next to two girls. The girls' whooping, applejack accent betrayed their origins in the south of Russia. They were both attractive in a provincial Soviet fashion. One, a slender brunette with full lips, wore a brown, fitted jacket over a red dress; the other, a tall bleached blonde with a thick braid down to her waist, was dressed in a two-piece outfit—a short yellow skirt and a matching blouse.

"Hey, gorgeous girls," Simon said. "Where do you hail from?"

"From Kerch," replied the brunette.

"Where's that?" Vadim the Frog jumped in, playing along.

"Don't you know?" the blonde asked.

"No, tell me," Frog croaked out.

"In Crimea, duh," explained the brunette. "Where the Black Sea and the Sea of Azov come together."

Simon's urge to punish Igor became unstoppable.

"Listen, girls," he said. "How about joining us for some champagne and *zakuski*?"

The girls from Crimea looked at each other and shrugged their shoulders.

"A good friend of ours is having a party just a few blocks from here," Frog chimed in, enjoying Simon's improvised performance. "I think you're going to like it."

"Okay, boys, but we can't stay too late," said the brunette and got up from the bench.

They headed back to Igor's house. When they got there, plates were being changed for dessert, and two couples were dancing in the far corner of the room. When they came in, many of the guests turned and stared. Misha and Tima disappeared behind the armoire, and Simon heard cascades of laughter. And then Sashenka walked in, carrying a birthday cake with candles. Behind her was Igor with a heavy pot of tea and a cake knife. Igor saw the two girls from Kerch who were now standing in the middle of the room, unsure of what to do or say, and his hand trembled, spilling tea on the rug.

"Girls, this the birthday boy," the Frog gleefully announced.

"Happy birthday!" said both girls in the jolliest of voices.

Igor's small eyes were drilling into Simon's face. He put down the pot and the knife, grabbed Simon by the elbow and dragged him out into the communal corridor.

"What are you doing?"

"Come on, man," Simon said, feeling the high of revenge pulse through his temples.

"Get these sluts out of here," Igor hissed, spewing saliva. "My parents will be here any minute."

"Okay, Igor, take it easy. I'll get them out," said Simon and went back to the room, where the two girls from Crimea were eating cake and drinking bubbly. Vadim the Frog was sitting between them, taking sips of cognac from a crystal tumbler and firing off rounds of drunken laughter.

"Girls," Simon leaned over and said in a conspiratorial voice. "Our friend, he's is acting crazy. I think it's unsafe for you to stay here. Why don't Vadim and I walk you back to the square?"

"Oh my God." The bleached blonde clasped her hands to her pink cheeks.

"Boys, it's okay," said the brunette, putting down her glass. "We'll show ourselves out."

Simon lifted his eyes and saw Sashenka, who was standing on the other side of the table and eyeing him.

Igor paced in the corridor the entire time, and only came back into the room after the girls from Crimea were gone. His forehead and upper lip were covered with perspiration. He loosened a knot of his red tie and poured himself a glass of warm vodka, guzzling it down and chasing it with a piece of meringue cake. A few minutes later his parents arrived. Igor's father demanded that all the guests toast his son's health, and the party resumed its interrupted course.

Two days later Simon left for a month of mandatory agricultural work at a collective farm an hour and a half outside Moscow. This was a form of penal servitude that the state imposed on university students and urban professionals, and it was difficult to dodge it. The popular Russian term for this month of slave labor was *na kartoshke*, which literally means "on potatoes"—

although they also picked apples, beets, and carrots, dug a trench for a new electrical cable, and even cleaned stables, joking about their "Herculean" tasks. For a month they lived in plywood cottages with one oil heater per room. They ate mostly noodles and rice with gloppy sauce and pieces of fat swimming in it, and at night they drank whatever rotgut they could lay their hands on.

The work itself wasn't very hard, and they sabotaged it whenever the supervisors looked the other way: stomping potatoes and carrots back into the soil; leaving unpicked apples under the trees; taking frequent smoking breaks. The hard part was the isolation. Misha and Igor were also picking potatoes at different locations, and only Tima was able to stay in Moscow by getting a doctor's note with the diagnosis of asthma.

While Simon was away, he got a letter from Sashenka, who called his home and got the rural postal address from his father. Simon never replied, nor did he call Sashenka upon his ascent from agricultural hell and return to Moscow. It was all over, especially after Igor's party.

Seven months went by. At the end of April 1987, on a spring afternoon, a telephone call was placed to their apartment from the Section of Visas and Permissions, and Simon's parents were told that their family was being allowed to emigrate. This came after almost exactly ten years as refuseniks. The Reznikovs quickly made arrangements to leave at the end of May.

A week before their departure, Simon invited about thirty friends over to a farewell party. He had been going through his address book, run across Sashenka's name and number, and called her.

"I heard from Saba. Congratulations," said Sashenka.

"I'm having a going-away party. Will you come, Sashenka?"

"Of course. Do you need any help?"

"No, just come. I'd like to say goodbye. Lord knows when I'm going to see you again."

Sashenka had cut her hair to a bob. There was also something new in her whole demeanor. Simon barely had a chance to speak with her alone, but he remembered her somber eyes the color of pine bark in winter, and the first furrow of adulthood oscillating across her forehead. He felt a surge of tenderness for her. As he greeted the arriving guests, he wondered why he still felt this way about Sashenka after months of severed contacts.

The first two years in America were the hardest for Simon. He missed his friends desperately. At first he wrote to them every other week or sometimes once a week, long collective letters describing his courses and professors at Brown University, girls he was trying to date on campus, his first job at a coffee shop, his car—a lipstick-red Ford Granada, his first trip to New York . . . his discovery of America.

Misha and Tima teamed up to write replies, which included caricatures of themselves with naked women. Strangely enough, they never mentioned Igor in their letters, although Simon always started his own with, "Dear Brothers Misha, Tima, and Igor!" He didn't know what to think. Then he wrote Igor a separate letter pleading with him to explain the silence. Simon missed Igor—his toughness and decisiveness, also his street-smartness and loyalty. Igor never replied. Simon wrote another letter, a short one this time, thinking that the first one might have gotten lost or intercepted. Still no reply. Then, in the spring of 1988, he telephoned Misha at two o'clock in the morning East Coast time—back then one couldn't direct dial. It turned out Igor was being drafted into the military. Something in Misha's voice made Simon suspicious, some note of apprehension when he spoke about their mutual friend.

Then things got extremely busy for Simon. He was working full-time during the summer and gearing up to apply to graduate school. He stopped writing regular letters to Russia. Nostalgia, he was learning, was like an acute infection, and time and distance eventually cured it. Unless, of course, it turned into a chronic condition.

In May of 1989 a small miracle happened: Simon invited Misha to come to his Brown graduation, and Misha was allowed to travel to America. They hadn't seen each other for two years. Misha stayed for almost a month, and they ended up doing all the things they had longed to do together as Soviet teenagers—driving around New England, going to Manhattan, sitting in jazz lounges and cafés.

From Misha, Simon learned that Igor was drafted in March of 1988 and served beyond the Arctic Circle, in the Murmansk Province. He made sergeant in six months. Sashenka went up to visit him in the autumn of the same year. They were married in Moscow during Igor's furlough. Misha and Tima weren't invited to the wedding, but they knew some of the details from Saba and other mutual acquaintances. Life eventually corrects for what it deems necessary, Simon remembered thinking to himself.

On the day Misha was flying back to Moscow, Simon drove him from Providence to JFK. After waiting in the Aeroflot check-in line amid Soviets bringing home suitcases stuffed with the spoils of capitalism and fellow émigrés going back for the first time to visit family graves and places of first love, after surrendering Misha's two distended suitcases and a bandaged-up cardboard box containing a VCR, Misha and Simon found a bar close to the gate and stopped for a glass of beer.

"Whew," Misha said, wiping his brow and taking a sip. "It's going to be a long flight."

"Transatlantic," Simon said, feeling the hollowness of his words.

"The *suki* at customs will probably turn my luggage inside out."

"It can't be as bad as when we were leaving Moscow."

"Almost as bad," Misha replied.

"I'll miss you," Simon said and put his right hand on Misha's shoulder. "I don't have such friends here."

Misha took off his glasses, cleaning the lenses with a corner of his white shirt and hiding sudden tears.

"By the way, I never told you this," Misha said, putting his John Lennon glasses back on. "Igor and I had a fight in Pärnu about a week after you arrived from the expedition."

"A fight?" Simon asked in disbelief. "What happened?"

"You were out with Sashenka. We bought a bottle of Estonian vodka, smoked herring, and bread, and set out for the jetty. It was Igor's idea to walk to the end and drink vodka at sunset. Tima and I agreed, don't ask me why. It was always like that with the three of us when you weren't around. We walked halfway to the end of the jetty, and then it got windy and cold, and it looked like a storm was brewing. I asked Igor to turn back. He wouldn't hear of it—'Man up, what's your problem?'—the usual. I said it was dumb to continue. Tima was just standing there silently, hands in the pockets of his wide trousers. 'Come on, you sissies,' Igor yelled. I told him again that it was a stupid idea to walk on the wet rocks. So he turned to me and wacked me on the face, and my glasses fell on the rocks. One lens broke. Thank God I had another pair at the house."

"Fucking fascist!" Simon said. "Why didn't you say anything?"

"I just didn't, that's all. What would you have done? Get in a fight with him? What's the point?" Misha replied.

"So how did you make up?"

"He came home late at night, all wet like an abandoned wolf cub, and I honestly felt bad for him. He apologized to me and to Tima, and things went back to normal. Sort of."

"I had no idea Igor had such a violent streak," Simon said.

"Now you do," Misha said, and unzipped his jacket pocket to check his boarding pass and red passport.

They finished their beers and snacks, and Simon took Misha to the gate. As he watched his friend step through the exit doorway, he thought of the day he left Moscow for good—passing through the turnstile of Soviet passport control and turning to take one last glance at his disappearing world.

Two more years passed. Simon was now a second-year doctoral student. This was still before the advent of email or Skype, but he and Misha now spoke on the phone about once a month. From Misha he heard that Sashenka, Igor, and Igor's parents had moved to America and were living in Queens, New York. They never called him, and he never sought contact with them, either. At first he followed their lives from a distance.

By the early 1990s a slew of kids from their old Pärnu crowd had emigrated and mainly settled in Tel Aviv, Berlin, New York, and Boston. Simon saw them periodically, and this was how he got sporadic news about Sashenka and Igor. They were still living in Forest Hills: Igor drove a cab, Sashenka was working in IT. They were childless. . . . And then, totally out of the blue, came Sashenka's e-mail . . .

She was living in a condo in West Hartford, an affluent and conspicuously Jewish area. After getting off the highway, Simon passed two synagogues on the way to her place. Groups of Jews were walking to shul. Women and young girls wore ankle-length skirts. Men in fedoras or derbies carried embroidered pillows under their arms. Driving through Sashenka's new neighborhood, Simon thought of a life of stability and tradition.

He parked his beat-up Subaru in front of Sashenka's condo complex and walked up to the front door. Her gendered Slavic name, Mironova, which she had never changed, looked foreign amid the wreath of markedly Jewish names such as "Goldstein" and "Rubin." He pressed the buzzer, and almost immediately he heard her voice, small and a bit husky, sounding as though it came from across the Atlantic Ocean.

"Syoma, *eto ty*?"

Not many people now called him by this tender diminutive.

"Yes, Sashenka, it's me."

"Come on up."

He ran up the carpeted stairs to the third floor. Sashenka was standing in the doorway, resting her head and left shoulder against the half-opened wooden door that she held with her right hand. She was smiling, a fretful smile. Her wheaten hair was long and straight, and both her eye shadow and lipstick were of the same opaque, redbrick color. Sashenka's ribbed oatmeal turtleneck, black stretchy pants and suede tassel loafers gave her a decidedly un-Russian look—perhaps a New England yuppie with a dash of preppiness. And yet there was something ethereal about Sashenka, as though the forces of gravity didn't have a firm grip on her slender frame.

Simon and Sashenka kissed and hugged each other. A wave of her perfumed hair washed over his cheek. Her fingers ran down his spine like a pianist's over a keyboard.

"Well, well, Sashenka. How long has it been?"

"Almost nine years. Come this way."

She led him through the foyer into a bright living room, furnished with light wood furniture that made the space look bigger. A white leather couch and a matching armchair stood near the window. He saw a cobalt blue coffee set on a low table, and a large, overflowing ashtray in the shape of a flatfish. Sashenka went to the kitchen and returned with a carafe of coffee. They sat down on the sofa.

"I want to hear all about you."

"You will," Sashenka said. "But, first, I wanted to tell you that I read your essay in the *Criterion*. I was in the local Barnes & Noble browsing in the magazine section and saw your name on the cover."

"The one about Felix Gregor?"

"Yes, the writer from Prague. I hadn't heard of him before."

"He's my guy," Simon said and nodded. "Going to be a book."

"When did you go to Prague?" Sashenka asked him.

"Spring of '93. Three years ago."

"You've come a long way, Simon Reznikov," Sashenka said without irony in her voice. "Writing in English. Ivy League universities. When you're a famous professor, I'm going to tell everyone that I knew you at tender nineteen."

"With this job market, let's hope I become a professor at all."

"You will—you've always known what you wanted from life. People like you get what they deserve."

This sounded bitter, but Simon knew Sashenka didn't mean it like that.

She put a piece of crumbly blueberry cake on his plate.

"I baked it last night. I've only started to cook again since I moved up here from New York. It's a strange feeling to be cooking just for yourself."

"I know," Simon said. "I've been doing it since I started graduate school. Now, tell me about coming to America. What happened to you guys?"

"Where to start . . . ?" She lit a thin brown cigarette. "You probably heard from good old Misha Tyshler and Saba and various others how Igor and I got married."

"I heard some things and had to work out the rest."

"I don't expect you to understand."

"I actually do understand it perfectly well. Igor was in the military. You went to rescue him. It's classic."

"And stupid. You had emigrated. I was in some sort of daze when I went to see him while he was in the army and later when he was home on furlough for the wedding. Igor took care of all the arrangements. His parents were dead set against it, telling him I would be like a 'rock tied to his neck.' That I was trying to snag a nice Jewish boy."

The phone rang. Sashenka let it ring until the answering machine picked up, but the caller didn't leave a message. Simon took off his shoes and stretched his legs on the coffee table.

"I'll be right back," Sashenka said. "This is going to take a while."

She came back from the bedroom with a velvet pillow that she placed under the nape of his head.

"After Igor was demobilized in the summer of 1990, we rented a studio— near the Sokol metro stop—so as not to stay with his parents. For a few months things weren't too bad, but then Igor's parents finally decided to emigrate, and Igor said we were going too. It was easier for him—he wasn't leaving his entire family behind in Moscow. We left in the fall of '91, on a drizzly October morning. I couldn't stop crying, and Igor was angry with both me and his parents."

"I remember that day very well," Simon said quietly. "I mean, I remember the day we left Moscow. It was awful: the airport; border control; all of you guys waving from the other side. My parents' friends. My mom wept the whole time."

"At least you got to leave with your parents. I . . ."

"I know," Simon said. "I mean, I don't know," he added guiltily.

"It was pretty horrible."

Sashenka continued with her story.

"We arrived in New York in November and went to live in Queens. Igor's father had an older sister in Forest Hills. We lived in a two-bedroom apartment together with Igor's parents. I got a data entry job and took evening computer classes for a year. Then I started working at a bank, and things were going pretty well for me professionally. For two years I pretty much supported them. I was making a good salary, really, and at first I didn't mind being the breadwinner. Igor's parents could speak no English. His mother did some clothes alterations and . . ."

"Sure," Simon interrupted. "I remember she used to do that back in Moscow. Whenever Misha and I would come over, she would always be knitting a sweater for a client or fixing a cuff or a lining. That's the main thing I remember about her. That and her pelican eyes."

Sashenka looked at him with surprise.

"Igor's father couldn't find professional work, so he began to clean offices and restaurants with a crew of other Russians. He started drinking heavily, and when he was drunk, he would call me 'shiksa' and 'Russian slut.' Igor's mother just looked away, racing her sewing machine. If Igor happened to be home at the time, he would stick up for me and threaten to break his dad's neck if he didn't shut up. But later, when we were alone, he told me that I provoked his father and that he was losing his mind 'between the hammer and the anvil.' And at other times when Igor's father got wasted, he—the father—would kiss my hands, get down on his knees, and ask me to forgive him. Can you believe it?"

"Yes. No," Simon replied, trying not to blush, as he felt responsibility for this *shikker*, as his paternal grandmother would call a Jewish drunkard. Responsibility and also shame.

"It was awful, just awful!" Sashenka said after pouring herself a little more coffee from the carafe. "I begged Igor to get our own apartment, and we eventually moved out. Igor was barely on speaking terms with his father by this point. The worst of it was that Igor refused to finish college—and he would have had only two more years to go if he had transferred his credits from Moscow. Didn't you do that?"

"Correct. They even counted Marxist-Leninist philosophy towards my electives," Simon replied, guile in his voice. "But that was at Brown."

"Well, he was going to go to Queens College," Sashenka sighed. "I implored him. He was terrified of failure, of not being able to compete with American students. You know how strong-willed he used to be when you were still friends."

"All of us used to think he had iron will and nerves of steel," Simon said, piling one Russian cliché on top of the other.

"Well, it's as if he had left his willpower in Moscow," Sashenka said.

"Sashenka, this happens to many immigrants."

"But it didn't have to happen to us."

She got up from the sofa and threw a white fluffy shawl over her shoulders.

"So we lived this way for three more years. I was working and making quite a bit of money. Igor began to drive a cab, mostly at night, and during the day he slept, read . . ."

"What did he read?" Simon asked, interrupting Sashenka again.

"Mainly the classics—Tolstoy, Turgenev, Goncharov. And lots of Bunin. You were crazy about Bunin when we met."

"*The Life of Arseniev* was one of my favorite novels," Simon answered dreamily. "But I can't read it now. The same with Hesse."

"My tastes have also changed here. Or is it age? In any case, when he wasn't working, Igor read a lot and watched Russian films on video. And he also hung out with a couple of Russian pals who, like himself, were having a hard time adjusting to their new lives. We didn't see much of each other during the week. I would be out of the apartment by seven thirty, and Igor's night shift usually began at six in the evening. We did try to do things together on weekends when he wasn't working. I remember, one time, we went to Vermont to ski."

"When did you learn to ski?" Simon asked.

"I didn't. I mean, I didn't that time. On the way up there we got into a huge fight in the car over something trivial, and Igor ended up skiing alone while I sat in our motel room, smoked, and watched TV for two days."

Sashenka lit another cigarette, then continued.

"There isn't much else to tell, I'm afraid. We grew farther and farther apart, going for months without making love. He was too proud to ask for it, and I was too withdrawn to seduce him, even though sex could sometimes mend things between us. I tried to get pregnant, but nothing came of it. I guess our marriage just wasn't meant to be from the very beginning. Doomed. I wanted us to move to a suburb, but he wouldn't hear of it. By the autumn of last year our conversations had been reduced to a mere formality. Then I had an affair with a French guy at work—a very nice guy, really, and it gave me strength. I knew I had to leave Igor."

"How did he take it?" Simon asked.

"At first he was livid. Then he started saying all these self-deprecating things, blaming everything on himself. He wanted to work things out, he said. It was too late, I told him. I already had a lawyer filing papers for divorce. And I got a great job offer from the First Bank of Hartford. I'm director of systems administration."

"That sounds prosperous. Did he try to get you to pay alimony?"

"No, he's not like that. Igor has many problems, but he does have a noble soul."

"I see," Simon said, bemused. It had been a long time since he had heard anyone use this expression. "A noble soul, hmm . . . yes, that and a heart of gold."

"Don't be sarcastic, please, Syoma. And you've hardly told me anything about your personal life."

"Pry away, Sashenka, it's not a secret," Simon answered.

"Okay, why aren't you married?" Sashenka asked, anxiety seeping into her voice.

"People get married later here. Plus I've been in graduate school. Not exactly a time to start a family."

"In America, perhaps. Not in Russia," Sashenka said.

"I'm more American now. Nine years it's been."

"No you're not, Syoma, trust me. You're still a nice Jewish boy from Moscow. The kind we all wanted to meet."

Simon was tempted to ask about her use of the collective "we" but held back. Sashenka got up, walked to the French doors and pressed her forehead to the glass. Silver-grey squirrels were madly chasing each other on the sloping lawn outside Sashenka's condo.

"That's a whole other conversation," Simon said, looking past Sashenka at the trunk flares of an American oak which stood at the edge of the back yard.

"I've dated, of course," he finally said. "But nothing serious."

"Nothing?" Sashenka asked.

"Well, almost nothing. An almost Central-European romance, and an almost North-American marriage," Simon replied.

He cleared this throat and told Sashenka about Milena Krupičková and the time he spent in Prague in the spring of 1993—his Bohemian spring. Sashenka listened without interrupting him. Simon finished the part about going with Milena on a trip to Marienbad. He started telling Sashenka about inviting Milena to America when she drew a sine wave across the palm of his open right hand and said:

"Let me make some more coffee. It will only take a few minutes. This new machine grinds coffee directly into a filter. Real fast. Remember how we used to sit in that café in Pärnu and drink Estonian coffee with chicory?"

"The one on the square near the mud baths?" Simon asked.

"Yes, what was it called? 'Daisies' or something like that. And we would all drink watery coffee with sweet, cheese pastries and dream about a cup of good, strong coffee. Be right back, Syoma."

Sashenka lit another long brown cigarette, took a puff, and walked across the living room to the open kitchen, the cigarette in her left hand, the empty carafe in her right one.

Simon leaned back on the sofa, closed his eyes, and recalled reading Milena's note on the plane from Prague. Sashenka brought in a carafe of fresh coffee.

"So, let's see, Syoma. You invited her to visit?"

"She said she couldn't imagine living away from home."

"I can understand that," Sashenka said.

"Don't you think it's a bit different?" Simon said, taking a piece of crumbly cake with his index finger and thumb and placing it in his mouth.

"Are you still in touch?" Sashenka asked, like a bather feeling the water with her uncurled toe.

"When my piece about Felix Gregor, the one you read, was published, I mailed her a copy of the magazine. She wrote back, a very formal letter. She was getting married. To her former boyfriend, who, by the way, is a musician and very jealous."

"So it wasn't a problem she wasn't Jewish?" Sashenka asked.

"I don't know. ... I probably didn't think so."

Simon hesitated, then added: "I thought we had so much in common."

"And now?"

"Now what?"

"Would it be an issue if you now met a non-Jewish woman and things became serious?"

"Sashenka, I'm not sure why you're asking me that?" Simon's fingers drummed out a trochaic beat on the coffee table.

"Just curious, I guess," Sashenka replied. "Back in Russia, you also said it wasn't an issue for you," she added.

"Did I really say that?" Simon asked.

"In Pärnu, we were walking on the beach. All the other girls in your gang of friends were Jewish. And most of the guys. So after two weeks I finally mustered up the courage and asked you."

"Asked me?"

"Asked you if I could ever fit in? Tima Obnorsky and I were the only non-Jews."

"I've totally and completely forgotten about this," Simon said. "Back in Russia it wasn't really an issue when it came to friends and lovers. But here it's become one ..."

"So you *have* changed, Syoma," Sashenka said plaintively.

The sunlight was no longer falling into the room. Outside, a brook looped its way through the gnarled feet of the old elm trees. On the manicured lawn, young crocuses were shooting up white and lilac.

"I like it here so much," Sashenka said, letting out a long wisp of smoke. "It's very peaceful. I never thought I'd enjoy being alone. Anyhow, we should probably get a bite to eat. I know a good lunch place only a few minutes from here."

They drove in Sashenka's brand-new Saab to a little restaurant overlooking a lake and a pine grove. Families with small kids sat eating their lunches, unhurriedly and contentedly, and to their parents Sashenka and Simon probably looked like a young couple testing the waters of married life. After lunch the two of them made a full circle around the lake, and Simon told Sashenka more about his immigrant years in America, and also about the books he was hoping to write. He mentioned his engagement to Nora Schermann, the wedding plans, and the breakup. Of course, Simon thought, these were only *stories* to Sashenka, stories as fictional and as distant from her as the ones she might read in novels or see in movies; whereas her life with Igor was as real to Simon as his own life.

As they completed their circle around the lake, Simon noticed a man in his fifties, dressed in baggy jeans and a windbreaker, who was cleaning his glasses with a soft cloth. A large spotted dog was sitting at the man's feet, looking at him with devotion.

"Great dog," Simon said to the man. "So calm. What kind is he?"

"She's a Newfoundland," the man replied, putting on his glasses. "She has a bad leg. So she mostly sits."

When Sashenka and Simon were at a safe distance from the dog owner, Simon said:

"I thought he had a Russian accent."

"You could be right," Sashenka replied.

"That guy could be me in twenty years," Simon said.

They were standing near an empty playground with three sets of swings, a sandbox, and a seesaw. A menagerie of clouds was drifting west over their heads—kangaroos, bears, elephants, and even a fat boa constrictor. The red bobber of a boy's fishing line was going up and down on the lake's steel surface. In the pine grove a woodpecker was keeping time with the bobber's convulsions.

"Listen, Sashenka."

Simon broke the silence, feeling an upswell of something hidden in the depths of memory.

"This may not be a good time to say it, but I may never again get myself to do it. I'm sorry I was such an arrogant bastard back in Russia. I'm sorry I treated you badly. I thought I was playing at chivalry. I didn't know any better at the time. Forgive me if you can."

"Syomochka, I forgave you a long time ago. I just wish it was you I got to leave Moscow with."

They looked at each other and smiled when they saw the tears in each other's eyes. They hugged and stood there on the lakeshore, gently stroking each other's backs and shoulders. Over the heads of Simon and Sashenka, a flock of Canada geese carried their shrieks of longing to the north.

They drove back to Sashenka's place, and Simon helped her make a simple dinner: twice-baked chicken (his mother's Moscow recipe), roasted potatoes and onions, and a mesclun salad with grape tomatoes and crumbled blue cheese. While the food was cooking, they sat on the sofa, arms over each other's shoulders, and drank a bottle of Chianti that had a faint, strawberry nose. A plaid, wool blanket covered their feet. The phone rang several times, but Sashenka ignored it. After supper they went back to the sofa, sat next to each other, drank jasmine tea, and ate thin sugar biscuits with apricot preserves. They reminisced about Russia, about their childhood and student days . . .

Then it was time for Simon to drive back to New Haven.

"How are you parents keeping?" Sashenka asked as Simon prepared to leave.

"Quite well, actually. Mama has a ton of violin students. Papa works for a biotech company in Cambridge as a senior staff scientist. And he still writes plays. He has a new one opening at this cool theater in St. Petersburg. I see them twice a month, sometimes more."

"You're so lucky," Sashenka said, straightening the collar of his denim jacket. "I haven't seen my dad in two years."

"Sashenka, promise you will call if you need anything," Simon said, changing the subject.

"Cross my heart," Sashenka said. "Would you like me to wrap you a piece of cake for the road?"

"Of course I would. And come to see me in New Haven," Simon said. "I won't be there for much longer. I'm waiting to hear from the places I interviewed with. Who knows where I'll end up going? Flagstaff, Arizona? Laramie, Wyoming? A campus at the end of the world?"

"There is no end of the world in America," Sashenka said.

When he was walking out the door, he turned around and asked her, "Do you still have the poem I wrote for you? I was just curious."

"Funny you should ask. Igor ripped it up, back in Moscow. I was so furious. He said he wanted nothing to do with you."

"Oh, well, good riddance," Simon said.

"I loved it, I still remember most of it."

"And our picnic on Misha Tyshler's twentieth birthday?" Simon asked.

"Silly boy, of course I do," said Sashenka with passion. "All of you: Misha; Igor; you; and chubby Tima had hard-ons when you were getting out of the water. God, I was eighteen. We were practically children."

"I thought Tima was sleeping under a willow tree," Simon said, and they both started laughing.

Simon hugged Sashenka and kissed her on the forehead.

"Remember," he said, pressing his hands to her cheeks and looking into her eyes. "Back in Russia, I once told you we would always be special friends. Summertime romance sometimes bonds people for life."

"Bye, Syoma. Drive carefully. Bye."

Simon drove back to New Haven on an empty highway, recalling details of that last blissful Estonian summer. He then remembered that during his first months in America, when nostalgia would ripple across his heart, he used to think, not without jealousy, that Igor had taken his place in their brotherhood of Moscow friends. But he was wrong, he now understood: Igor hadn't taken his place, but had faded away into oblivion, first vanishing from Simon's own life, then from Sashenka's . . .

During the next two weeks Simon telephoned Sashenka two or three times, only to talk to her answering machine, and then things got crazy with the job search. At the end of April, after he had accepted a tenure-track position at a women's college west of Boston, where a famous compatriot of his had taught during the war, he drove up to visit his parents and search for an apartment. Simon was meeting his cousin Yuri, now in charge of his own real estate agency, who talked him into looking at a couple of one-bedrooms in Brookline, even though Simon could hardly afford to buy in that area. He arrived too early and went into a Russian bakery-café on Beacon Street to kill half an hour. The proprietress, a turtle with the dovish eyes of an Odessan belle, asked him where he came from in the old country and what his *biznes* was in Boston. After Simon had introduced himself with the affected cordiality that he sometimes poured on fellow émigrés—in the sense that it's wonderful to see other Russians in a strange land—the turtle-dove said she used to know his mother's half-sister during her days in the Bolshoi Ballet. She served Simon a glazed poppy seed roll on the house and wouldn't stop talking about his aunt's gorgeous legs. Simon ended up scribbling down his parents' number on a napkin just to be rid of the proprietress and settled down with a Russian daily newspaper near a rain-speckled window. He was almost finished with his glass of green tea when his eyes wandered across a short article about a cab driver who had murdered his ex-wife outside her apartment building in West Hartford.

BORSCHT BELT

In 1988, at the end of May, Simon Reznikov turned twenty-one. Having reached the legal drinking age for the second time (it was eighteen in the Soviet Union), he felt that immigrant time was moving forward while also flowing backward. Simon and his parents celebrated his birthday in the tower of a fairy-tale castle overlooking Narragansett Bay. Having already been new Americans for ten months, the Reznikovs had become well versed in the geography of Rhode Island and Providence Plantations. And they had already been to Boston at least three times, and to New York City once. These great cities beckoned them, former Muscovites, with the promise of deliverance from their providential existence, where Simon's father was cut off from the Russian literary community and his mother from a big city's music scene, and where Simon pined after his world of Moscow friends.

After moving back home from campus, Simon spent a week looking for summer jobs. He needed to save up enough money to pay for the two months he was planning to spend in France the following summer, between college and graduate school. One job fell into his hands from a dormmate who had been waitressing at the Brown Faculty Club and took him to meet the manager.

"Can you balance a wine bottle on a tray?" asked the manager during the interview. In the 1970s, she had been crowned Providence Beauty Queen.

"I can," Simon answered, his prior restaurant experience limited to working at a coffee shop.

He got the job, purchased a white shirt, polyester black trousers, and an adjustable bowtie at Sears on Main Street, and joined the motley brotherhood and sisterhood of the Faculty Club waitstaff. The group included the Portuguese common-law wife of a Jewish chef, a twin brother and sister whose Polish parents ran a funeral parlor in southern Rhode Island, a melancholy Puerto-Rican girl who was majoring in urban planning and had a Coca Cola dependency, and a charismatic bearded drifter from Pittsburgh who zestfully recited the tsar's titles. Emperor and Autocrat of All Russia . . . Tsar of

Astrakhan . . . Tsar of Georgia . . . Prince of Estland . . . Lord of Turkestan . . . Duke of Schleswig-Holstein, and so forth. The tips at dinners and weddings were generous, but the former Miss Providence demanded the kind of daily adoration Simon couldn't muster. And so he wasn't getting enough work at functions.

A trail of job ads and phone interviews brought him to The Bonnets, a private beach club on Narragansett Bay, where a pair of Providence restaurateurs ran an overpriced summer steak-and-lobster establishment. For some reason, the owners hired Simon on the spot, probably calculating that after a day of sun and sea the WASP-y clients would mistake his lack of garrulousness for dry European humor and take pleasure in his "Boris-and-Natasha" accent. The owners, who made their waitstaff lie about "fresh swordfish" (frozen) or "fresh tarragon" (dried), were correct about Simon's appeal to the beach club clientele. He was rewarded with extra tips for sporting dark underwear under unlined off-white slacks, for mixing up the words "swim" and "bathe" (as in "I bathed twice today, the water is lovely"), and for answering affirmatively to their patronizing questions.

"Aren't you glad you're in America?" the tipsy diners would ask him.

"Very glad," he replied, almost sincerely.

For all of June and July Simon worked two restaurant gigs, the Faculty Club and The Bonnets, coming home at two in the morning. He had no time to write or just be, and only the thought of seeing Paris the following summer kept him going. As July drew to a close, Simon's parents started to worry that he was wasting his best years.

"Asking rich boors how they would like their steak cooked—that's your idea of a summer?" Simon's father exploded.

"You're not having a normal summer," his mother said, adding fuel to the fire.

"That's not what student years are supposed to be like," said his father. "Is that why we brought you to America—so you would work and work and save and save? Like a perfect little philistine."

"You need adventure," his mother intoned. "At your age—"

"Yes, at my age. . . . Well, where can I go at my age?" Simon shot back, not angrily but despondently.

After less than a year in America they hadn't yet discovered Cape Cod, and Simon knew that he didn't want to go on a beach vacation to Narragansett with his parents.

Enter Simon's childhood friend Styopa (Steve) Agarun. Styopa's and Simon's parents had been friends in Moscow since the late 1960s. Styopa was less than a year Simon's senior, and treasured photographs showed Simon at two months lying in Styopa's crib and clawing a stuffed rabbit. In 1970, their families vacationed together outside Sebastopol. They shared a squalid cottage, and Simon vaguely remembered the panic among the vacationers as rumors of the cholera outbreak in the south of Russia had reached Crimea.

As long as Simon could remember Styopa, his friend's appearance was exuberantly Middle Eastern. Next to Styopa, Styopa could pass for a Slavic boy. When their parents sent Styopa and Simon to a young pioneer summer camp, the kids taunted Styopa as both a Jew and a *chuchmek*, a slur applied to non-Russians from Central Asia and the Caucasus. Simon's own plight as simply a Russian Jew was considerably better. Styopa's father came from the Mountain Jews, a mysterious Jewish tribe of the Caucasus. Styopa, his father, and his grandparents all had anthracite hair and eyebrows, olive skin, dark-brown eyes with a prunish sheen, and if you didn't know their true origins, you could have mistaken them for Persians or Kurds. Styopa's grandfather had retired as an air force lieutenant colonel; he kept a collection of daggers and rifles on the walls of his den and ruled the family with the fierceness of an elder in a besieged mountain village-fortress. Styopa was in fact a diminutive of Stepan, not exactly a first name favored by Russian Jews, and yet the retired ace insisted that his grandson bear the name of a seventeenth-century Cossack rebel.

By the time the twelve-year-old Styopa and his family had left Moscow for good, the grandfather was gone, and only his widow, an accountant, carried the family's Mountain Jewish legacy to America. Had the warrior grandfather been alive, the Agarunovs would have certainly made *aliyah* instead of settling in Boston. The Agarunovs and the Reznikovs applied for exit visas around the same time, except that Styopa's family got out and Simon's got stuck in refusenik's limbo.

When they arrived in Rhode Island almost ten years later, Styopa and Simon only had their childhood memories in common. Styopa was an American product: a Bostonian; a Red Sox fan; an admirer of Ronald Reagan. He was only in some ways still a Jew from the USSR: he majored in computer science at Boston University and lived at home throughout college. To Simon and his parents, this bashful twenty-two year old working for a tech start-up in Cambridge was still the old Styopa whom Simon used to tease on an overcrowded Crimean beach. And one more thing: Styopa persuaded his father to shorten their last name to Agarun and Americanize their first names. Thus, Stepan Agarunov became Steve Agarun, and Doktor Marat Gavriilovich Agarunov became Dr. Mark Agarun . . .

On that particular day in the beginning of August, Styopa had driven down to Providence for a visit. They were sitting on the balcony of the Reznikovs' rental apartment overlooking a fire station, and Simon was telling his childhood friend how it was summer, he had no vacation plans of his own, and this would have never happened back in Moscow. Styopa listened silently as a fire engine backed into the garage, moaning like an old gigolo.

"I got it," Styopa suddenly said, slapping himself on the thigh. "You should go to Bluebell Inn."

"Where's that?" Simon asked.

"In the Catskills."

"The Castiles?" Simon compulsively punned. "All the way in Spain?"

"Hilarious, Syoma. Not the Cas-*teels* but the Cat-*skills*. In Upstate New York," Styopa replied, unperturbed. "They used to call it the 'Borscht Belt.'"

"Why the hell 'Borscht Belt?'" asked Simon.

"There used to be a lot of Jewish resorts there," Styopa explained.

"'Borscht Belt' doesn't sound Jewish at all," Simon said. "Russian, Ukrainian, but not Jewish."

"Well, perhaps to you it doesn't," Styopa conceded. "But here it used to sound Jewish. Like Jewish deli food. So the name stuck."

The story Styopa told him began with a senior colleague of his father, a Jewish radiologist at Brigham and Women's. He had grown up in Queens and every summer used to go with his family to Bluebell Inn, a Jewish resort in the Catskills. The radiologist had shared nostalgic anecdotes about this place, and he was still friendly with the owners. He was the one who convinced Styopa's parents that Bluebell Inn would be a good place to ship off Styopa's grandmother with fourteen-year-old Styopa and his three-year-old brother Josh.

"We first went to the Catskills in the summer of 1980. When you had the Olympics."

"We?"

"Well, you had the Olympics. We had the boycott."

"Why not Cape Cod, then?" Simon asked. "Isn't it where you Bostonians summer?"

"We were new to the area," Styopa clarified. "Renting a house for a month was expensive. Papa was repeating residency. The Catskills just made sense at the time. And then we became attached to it. "

The Agaruns didn't just get used to sending their children and grandmother to the Catskills. Styopa made himself indispensable to the owner of Bluebell Inn, an ageing Jewish woman who ran the resort like a small principality. Styopa (already Steve) had started out as a bellhop. He was soon elevated to a jack-of-all-trades, pool caretaker, and executive assistant to the owner. Eventually he ran the Bluebell Inn during the summer months.

"Was the pay good?" Simon asked.

"The first summer the lady paid me nothing. Just room and board in exchange for work. Plus tips. Still by the end of August I had a wad of cash, mostly dollars but also fives and tens. Like in a gangster movie. This thick," and Styopa made a square bracket with his thumb and index finger. "Eventually, Mrs. Roots, the proprietor, started paying me and also let us stay for free. She loved my brother Josh."

"So why did you stop going?"

"It got a little complicated," Styopa said and lowered his gaze.

"Complicated?" Simon pressed, still a champion of clarity.

"I was in college already. Mrs. Roots sold the place to a Russian couple from New York, the Kosolapovs. By then the place had become like a little Odessa in the mountains. I worked for them one summer—after my sophomore year—and it was different. And then something happened. . . . I'll tell you another time."

Styopa's eyes became misty, his long eyelashes fluttering like dragonflies.

"So, Castiles, I mean, Catskills," Simon said. "So be it. Can you come with?"

"During the week I can't."

"What do you expect? Me to go alone?"

"No, not alone. Take the grandmothers. And I'll come for the weekend."

"I'm not sharing a room with any grandmother."

"You don't have to," Styopa replied, sanguine. "You will have what's called a split. Two connecting rooms, and a shower with doors on either side."

The following day Styopa, who possessed a talent for combinatorics, had the whole plan figured out, and both sets of parents had signed off on it. He telephoned Bluebell Inn and made reservations. Simon's maternal grandmother, who had left Ukraine as a young woman and spoke Russian like a true Muscovite, and Styopa's Mountain Jewish grandmother who swallowed whole Russian consonants like apricots, pits and all, weren't exactly close friends. But they had known each other for decades and agreed to go on the Catskills sojourn together.

This was going to be Simon's first American vacation. On the eve of departure, he lay awake, trying to visualize Styopa's resort. Back in the Soviet days, he heard stories from Jewish emissaries who came from America to visit refuseniks. A vague something about New York Jews creating a vacationland for themselves at a time when hotels had signs like "Near Churches," and Jews weren't welcome in many places. To a Moscow kid, Jewish colonies of summer cottages and hotels full of Yiddish speakers seemed like a fiction from a bygone era . . .

On the morning of their journey to the Catskills, armed with a set of AAA-issued maps, the route highlighted in poisonous orange, Simon picked up his grandmother from her apartment building across the street from Bread and Circus. She had turned seventy-four that summer and was fanatically learning English.

"I hope we meet some interesting people there," Simon's grandmother said as they left behind the outskirts of Providence.

"Interesting how?" Simon asked, just to nettle her a little bit.

"Interesting, educated people. Not like some of the double-dyed provincials in my building."

"*Babulya*," Simon said. "Maybe you'll meet a nice old gentleman."

"Not interested," his grandmother sliced. "Men my age are unreliable. I'd rather go to Paris."

In Boston they collected Styopa's grandmother from her apartment, also located, by some stroke of immigrant symmetry, across the street from an organic foods supermarket. The two grandmothers soon busied themselves with family talk while Simon drove, maps spread out on the passenger seat, through central Massachusetts, then Connecticut, finally picking up Interstate 95 at New Haven. This was only Simon's second long-distance motoring trip, and he was still giddy with the openness of American highways.

"Are we near George Washington Bridge?" Simon's grandmother asked as they approached Tappan Zee Bridge.

"No, this is a different bridge," Styopa's grandmother said with authority in her voice. "*Tap-on-Thee.*"

"Oh, that's too bad," sighed Simon's grandmother. "I really wanted to see George Washington Bridge."

Simon recounted a bittersweet anecdote about a Russian cab driver from New York. At the naturalization exam the man was asked to name the first US president. He answered: "George Washington Bridge." The examining African-American lady was going to fail him, but he mustered all his English and told her that he had been working his whole six American years, driving a cab, putting food on his children's table, never once was on public assistance, and was sorry he hadn't had time to study US history. The examiner rolled her eyes and spared the Russian cabbie.

"How embarrassing for him," said Simon's grandmother.

Styopa's grandmother only said "*nu i nu*" (which means "unbelievable" or "wow") and clasped and unclasped her purse.

They were already on the bridge; below, the Hudson coursed like the trunk of a biblical water animal. Straight ahead Simon could make out the contours of the town of Nyack, where, he had heard, White Russians had been living and burying their dead. After Tappan Zee, they got off the highway and drove north and west, first on a snaky, looping parkway, later switching to smaller roads. Despite the grandmothers' urgings to drive on, Simon stopped several times on the way to the resort. The towns they passed had such marvelous names: Goshen; Scotchtown; Bloomingburg. They made their last stop at the melodious-sounding town of Monticello, where Simon filled the tank of his voracious car, and insisted that they take a stroll up and down the town's main street. He wanted to treat the grandmothers to a cup of coffee and a piece of pie at a diner but they adamantly refused. As they were walking back to the car, Simon's eye caught sight of a very tall powerfully built man with a full head of greying hair and a thick brush of raven mustache. Where did I just see his face? Simon wondered. A rumpled shirt unbuttoned on his chest, the tall man was carrying two buckets of paint while talking, in Russian, to a teenage girl in a skimpy dress who looked like she didn't want to be there. For a brief moment Simon's eyes locked with the bottomless eyes of the mustached man, and he saw the frozen Neva, the dome of St. Isaac's at sunset, and the marble bodies of the Summer Garden's beauties boarded up for the winter months. Simon almost leapt out towards the big man and the girl but some new American force of self-restraint kept him in place.

"That man, I think he's a famous Russian writer," he said to the grandmothers already in the car.

"What would a Russian writer be doing here?" Styopa's grandmother said with authority. "You must have misheard. Polish, maybe. And he doesn't even look like a writer."

Styopa had told him to start paying attention after they passed the town of Liberty.

"When you enter Roscoe," Styopa said in Russian on the phone, "look for a big sign for Bluebell Inn on your left. Can't miss it."

They left Liberty behind and soon after that entered the town whose name Simon wasn't sure how to pronounce properly in English, all because of the "oe" cluster. *Ros-coy? Rose-cow?*

He would have missed the turn had it not been for Styopa's grandmother.

"Slow down, we're here," she yelled from the back seat. And there it was, the sign for Bluebell Inn Resort Hotel, and below, printed in two horizontal columns, were the words "restaurant•outdoor pool•ping pong | bar•entertainment•sports." And beneath those words there was a smaller sign for a place where hunting dogs were trained and pheasant hunting could be enjoyed. Simon thought of Levin and his gentle dog Laska, and his heart soared.

An uphill road with ruts and patches of grass in the middle brought their car to a sloping meadow, from which the resort's main building came into view. It was a three-story white chalet with a red roof and a row of garrets in the attic. Its porticoed front porch made Simon think of Bologna, where he and his parents had spent an evening during their Italian summer of transit. To the left of the main building, at the end of an overgrown path, a lake showed its unpolished silver through veiny malachite. Simon parked, then hauled their luggage to the main entrance.

"Where's the bellhop?" Simon's grandmother asked.

"What do you expect?" Styopa's grandmother replied with the disdain of a Mountain Jewish lioness. "Russian owners don't bother with such things. The place's positively going downhill."

They passed an older couple in matching bright-yellow shorts playing ball with a little girl. "Throw up ball, Mishellochka," the Russian grandparents were both screaming in English. "Throw up."

A woman in her mid-forties, a baby blue kerchief tied, bandana-style, across her perspiring forehead, stood at the reception counter like a captain on the bridge.

"Well, hello, dear guests," she said in Russian. "Welcome to Bluebell Inn," she added, in English. "A hot day," she said, switching back to Russian and blowing air at her face from under her tucked-in upper lip.

"Are you the Boston sisters? The Millershteyns?" the receptionist said to Simon's and Styopa's grandmothers. "You don't look alike."

"Different fathers," Simon added, unable to resist making the kind of joke they used to make in his old Russian circle of friends, always looking for a way to inject innuendo.

The receptionist located their reservations but was having trouble finding the one for Styopa's grandmother—Agarunova having been transformed to "Runova" and filed under "R." The *aga*—aha—part disappeared, like a stolen sigh. As they waited—both grandmothers pacing back and forth in the lobby, Simon tapping on the counter's wood that remembered the palms and fists of the hotel's thousands of clients—it became clear to him that staying in a connecting room with his grandmother would be a grave error.

"What's your name?" Simon whispered to the receptionist in a warm-hearted Soviet manner.

"Basya."

"Where are you from, esteemed Basya?" he asked again, bringing his face an inch closer to hers.

"Minsk."

"Minsk?" Simon said with glee. "We had an aunt in Minsk. Aunt Bronya. The only one who survived."

"My papa's whole family was in the ghetto," Basya said. "He returned home from the front an orphan. Oy, the pain, the pain," Basya sighed, dropping metal keys with wooden chain holders on the counter. She paused, then asked Simon: "You must be from Leningrad?"

"Moscow. But my dad's from Leningrad."

"Intelligentsia," Basya said, smiling broadly. "Probably demanding, too. Don't expect too much of this place."

"Basya," Simon said under his breath, leaning over the reception counter. "Any chance I could have a room of my own?"

"Don't want to be next to grandma, naughty boy," Basya shook her head.

"It's not that, I just—"

"I get it," Basya cut him off. "For the same price I can give your grandmother a regular room with a private bath. But you'll have to stay in the attic."

"The attic?"

"That's where our single service staff live. Small rooms, no frills. Bathroom in the hallway. But the view is spectacular."

"I'll take it, Basya."

Simon told his grandmother a half-lie about the connecting rooms being all taken, and she accepted it. Styopa's grandmother demanded a room "on the second floor at the far end of the corridor." Simon delivered the grandmothers' luggage, then ran up two flights of stairs to the attic. His low-ceilinged garret had a squeaky bed, a side table, a painted blue chair, and a wardrobe with a broken door. From the dormer window he could see the front lawn embroidered with vacationers, the undulating wall of the woods, and a tall glass of mountain sky cut with wispy clouds. This was, he reminded himself, his first American vacation, and things could only get better.

By the end of their first day in the Catskills, two things had become apparent. The resort was living out its past grandeur, and there were no adult American-born Jews left among its clients. All the adults and also some of the older kids staying at Bluebell Inn had been born in the Soviet Union—when it was already teetering but still standing. In some ways, the resort itself was like the country they had come from . . . drowning in the myths of its past.

Most of the vacationers came from the boroughs of New York and from New Jersey, and some from Philadelphia and even Baltimore. These were folks who had gotten out in the 1970s. Immigrants with ten, sometimes fifteen years of American life under their canvas belts and elastic bands, many of them had raised children here. Some had grandchildren with names like Benichka (from Benjamin) or Binochka (from Sabina). They hadn't tasted refusenik despair back in Russia but had had to fight their own immigrant battles in America. Most of the adult men and many of the women were conservative in a primordial fashion, the way steak is bloody and snake is slithery. The ex-Soviet Jews professed fist-brandishing Zionism without wanting to live in Israel. Most of the older men and some of the older women had been in the war against Germany and carried signs of battlefield injuries.

Dinner was served in the main dining room with plaintive ceiling fans and a view of the porticoed porch and the meadow. The menu included typical Russian appetizers like "herring under a fur coat" and typical American entrees like "veal parmesan."

Their server, introducing herself, said with pride: "My name's Regina. My mom's the chef here for the summer."

"And for the winter?" Simon tried to joke.

"She cooks at a restaurant in Queens."

"And you, what do you do during the year?" Simon asked.

"I go to high school during the year. In Forest Hills," answered the young woman, straightening her black apron. "For the main course?" she asked the grandmothers, switching to Russian.

Simon wolfed down his entree, followed by a serving of cherry compote and a slice of poppy seed roulette. Abandoning the grandmothers, as he would again and again during that Catskills vacation, he went out for a stroll. Almost everywhere he turned there was a feeling of decline—not the serene decay of an impoverished noble's estate but a loveless, breakneck ownership. Nets on the tennis courts hung like ripped stockings on the back of a bedroom chair. Boats tied to the neglected dock were missing oars, and half the lake's surface was patched over with duckweed. Paths hadn't been graded in a long time, and benches needed a facelift. Only the swimming pool looked renovated— a wealthy suburban reveler to the resort's wan pleasures.

Simon wandered the grounds, picturing in his head the way the place looked in its heyday. In his exalted imagination, émigrés of yore walked the paths and sat on the benches of an idyllic mountain enclave—lovers of art and philosophy, anarchists and labor socialists, starlets of Shanghai cabarets and inglorious Yiddish actresses, rabbis and militant Zionists . . .

He returned to the hotel just in time to observe his compatriots' evening rituals. The front lawn buzzed with Russian-American children and their parents or grandparents in colorful outfits and baseball hats. They were convinced that their offspring were better off frolicking on these unkempt lawns in the Russianized Catskills than by the shores of the Baltic or Black Sea.

Almost all of the rocking chairs lining the front porch were occupied by coteries of elderly Russian Jews. Simon was thinking of his childhood friend Styopa—Steve— Agarun as he crossed the meadow and approached the main entrance with its white fronton and peeling wooden columns.

"Young man, a very good evening to you," said a big female voice from behind one of the columns.

Simon stopped and turned sideways. Staring at him, slightly askance, was a lady in her seventies with long bare arms. Age hadn't clouded her cornflower blue eyes. The lady had permed copper hair, rouged cheeks, and long mascaraed eye lashes; a silk shawl covered her bare shoulders but revealed the décolletage of her dark floral dress. As Simon's eyes rolled down the lady's chin and neck to her cleavage, he could almost feel the evening moisture on curlicues of her drab skin.

"I believe you know my good friend Styopa," said the lady.

"He used to work here," Simon replied. "How do you—"

"My name is Madame Yankelson." The lady introduced herself with authority. Simon was instantly surprised by her use of the word "Madame" when speaking in Russian. "Violetta Arkadyevna Yankelson, but I want you to call me simply 'Violetta.'"

Leaning on the column with his right shoulder, Simon stood on the porch, both wanting and not wanting to leave, his eyes traveling back and forth between the meadow and Madame Yankelson, whom he had instantly given the nickname "Pique Dame."

"You and I will have a *roman*," said Madame Yankelson. "Platonic, of course," she added, noting his bewilderment.

Sitting in a rocking chair next to Madame Yankelson was another lady, beige and mothlike, clad in a brown dress with a beet-red belt. Madame Yankelson didn't introduce her to Simon. He would soon discover that this lady always sat with Madame Yankelson in the manner of a *demoiselle de compagnie*. She hardly ever spoke, a silent witness whose name, Simon learned eventually, was Lydia Shmukler. When she smiled, the lake's greenish patina quivered on the red gold of her upper teeth.

Back in those days of his American infancy, Simon still had the talent for sleeping late. In the morning, when he finally came down from his garret, breakfast was almost over. He bumped into the grandmothers as they were leaving the dining room, both of them wearing sundresses. Styopa's grandmother was grim; Simon's chipper.

Simon had breakfast in a baby-blue cotton robe with grey and yellow stripes. The robe was a birthday present and he was convinced it looked appropriate for a mountain resort. After consuming a generous helping of challah French toast and drinking two cups of sweet black tea with lemon, Simon went out onto the porch for a gulp of fresh air.

"Do you sleep in this?" a voice from behind his back asked in doubly accented Russian, interrupting Simon's reverie. He turned around to discover that the voice belonged to a stocky kid of about seventeen or eighteen with a head of sandy curls and daredevilish, hazel eyes.

"No, I just eat in it," Simon answered, a bit belligerently.

"How long have you been here?" the kid asked, switching to English.

"Second day," Simon replied.

"Not *here* here. In this country."

"A year."

"I see," the kid said and offered a hand in a handshake. "My name's Petya. I'm from Brooklyn. Kharkov, originally. We left when I was nine."

Simon introduced himself.

"A Muscovite. What brings you here?" Petya asked.

Simon explained about driving up with two grandmothers, and Petya just shook his head and cracked his knuckles.

"We started coming here eight, nine years ago with our families. Now the place is all Russian. Owners, too."

"Are you here with your folks?" Simon asked.

"My grandmother died earlier this year. And my younger brother is at sleepaway camp. So I'm solo this summer. Working as a pool attendant. Free room and board. Not too bad, huh?" Petya acted older than his age.

"Where do you go to college?" Petya asked.

"Brown. I transferred after we came here."

"I'd love to go to Brown. But I'll probably end up at Albany, maybe Stony Brook."

Simon didn't know what to say and just looked at his feet.

"I tell you what," Petya said, jerking his upper body like a stallion, "we'd love to pick your brain about college."

"We who?"

"There's a group of Russian kids here. Most of us are going to be seniors in high school; a few are going to college. Some work in the dining room, others run little kids' activities. Why don't you meet us later?"

"Sure," Simon said, and went back to his garret to throw on swimming trunks and a polo shirt.

By the time Simon, notebook in hand, came back from the pool, the Russian kids had already dispersed, leaving a circle of chairs at the far corner of the front porch.

"So I hear you met Petya," said their server Regina.

"Word travels fast around here," Simon replied.

"Yes it does. Come hang out with us," Regina replied with a chortle and walked back to the kitchen, hips shimmying under her black skirt.

After supper, Simon found Regina, Petya, and other boys and girls congregating at the far end of the long front porch.

"Hey, pull up a chair and join us," said Petya, who acted like the leader of this brotherhood and sisterhood of young ex-Soviet Jews. "Here, meet my friends. This is Pasha, our tennis guru. This is Anya—works with little kiddies. Now, this guy"—Petya pointed to a swarthy fellow with piggish eyes who made the Adirondack chair look too small—"this is Sam from Kishinev. He's training to be a sumo wrestler and is also the resident lawn cutter." Somnolent and silent, Sam would have mangled Simon's hand if he hadn't pulled it out. "And this is our star . . . our Marinochka. Beauty and brains. All the boys are in love with her."

The girl whom Petya introduced last was standing in the shadow of a corner column, her right leg slightly bent at the knee. She was wearing a sleeveless white shirt with see-through holes on the sides and black capri pants with ties at the bottom. One of the ties hung loose, and Marina's tennis shoes were also untied, their laces tucked in. Marina had small hands and feet, and when she looked at Simon and smiled just slightly, her full lips and her tongue formed a perfect trifolium. A night violet, Simon thought, remembering a turn of the century Russian poem his father admired and read to him. Marina's titian eyes, wide set, almost oriental, gave the illusion that she was looking at you and also at her own temples and beyond. There was mystery in this girl from Brooklyn, and Simon instantly wanted to be alone with her. The evening wore on as they hung out on the porch and Simon told the group about Brown—life on campus, courses and professors, and also some of the celebrities' children he had run across, among them Ringo Starr's stepdaughter and Candace Bergen's and Louis Malle's daughter.

"Do you only meet celebrity chicks?" Petya asked.

"I don't know," Simon answered, truthfully. "I don't think I've met sons of celebrities on campus."

Marina, who was still striking the same pose, except that the top of her body had been released from the column's shadow, moistened her lips and smiled, looking towards the front lawn.

All the while Simon was scanning the émigré sunset theater out of the corner of his right eye. An old gentleman with a carved cane, the collar of his white shirt worn over a cream-colored jacket with three rows of Soviet military ribbons, approached the two grandmothers who were strolling on the sunlit section of the meadow, arms folded behind their backs, in the manner of convicts in a prison courtyard.

"That's my grandfather," Marina said about the old gentleman with regalia.

"And that's my grandmother and my friend's," Simon added.

"He's casting a wide net," Petya commented.

"I feel like going for a stroll," Simon said, getting up. "Who wants to join me?"

"I'll go," Marina said, and their whole gang turned in her direction.

"Nice, preppy boy," Petya said without malice. "Your lucky night."

Marina and Simon walked across the footlights, stage, and backstage of the émigré theater, heading for the lake.

The last time Simon had interacted with a Russian girl had been a summer ago in Italy. Later, at Brown, he didn't know other Russian students, male or female. A Soviet immigrant on an Ivy League campus, he had trouble speaking the language of American love. Which is why encounters with the daughter of a senator from the southwest or the daughter of an Argentine-born cardiologist from Kansas City started with a promise of passion and ended with dejection. His Russian romantic ardor and his chivalry were mistaken for cultivated machismo. And it took a half-Irish, half-Jewish psychology graduate student from Chicago to figure him out, which is why they dated, clandestinely, for much of the spring as Simon also tried to write his first English-language stories.

Walking next to Simon on a willowy path wasn't just one Marina Ayzenbaum, a recent high school graduate staying at Bluebell Inn with her family and going off to Binghamton in the Fall. Walking next to him was an RGA, Russian Girl in America—Russian roots, Brooklyn breeding, and American ambitions all throbbing in her tenderly provincial speech.

Simon took hold of Marina's small manicured fingers. Over her left shoulder she glanced at the front lawn.

"My mom, she likes to spy on me," she said, trustingly. "She's over there, playing frisbee with my little sister."

"Is your father also here?" Simon asked.

"Only for the weekend. He likes to sit on the porch and smoke cigars after supper," Marina explained.

"That's pretty darn American of him," Simon said, but not facetiously.

As they stepped onto a mossy trail that girded the lake, he pulled Marina closer and put his right arm around her shoulders, his fingers touching the embroidered top of her blouse.

"Tell me about yourself," he asked her.

"There's not a whole lot to tell." Marina switched to English. "I was six when we came. We used to live in Zaporozhye. I don't remember very much."

Zaporozhye (or Zaporizhia) was a city in the southeast of Ukraine. Simon had never been to it in his twenty Soviet years, but he knew two principal things about the place of Marina's birth: it's on the Dnieper River and it's near the historic stronghold of Ukrainian Cossacks. The rest he had to imagine.

"My dad was an engineer and did something in construction," Marina told him as she fingered a blue cornflower. "Before college he used to drive a truck in the Soviet army, and he went back to driving a cab after we came to Brooklyn. He did that for five years, then he started a jewelry business with two friends from home."

"Successful?" Simon asked, picturing heavy necklaces and bejeweled hands.

"*T'fu-t'fu*," Marina replied in Russian, arching the tip of her tongue. "I sometimes help him at the store. But he usually doesn't want me to."

"Too dangerous?"

"It's not that. He wants me to become a lawyer. And he wants to sell his share of the business when he's sixty and retire in Florida."

"I also want to retire in Florida and live in Miami," Simon said, half joking.

"You do?" Marina looked at him in bafflement.

"What's Canarsie?" he asked, referring to Marina's home in Brooklyn. In Brooklyn he only knew three areas: Williamsburg, Brooklyn Heights and, naturally, Brighton Beach.

"Just another neighborhood," Marina replied.

Under the old weeping willow by a derelict boathouse they stood for a while, kissing, and Simon told her about the world he had left in Moscow.

"What would you want with a simple girl who doesn't even come from Moscow?" Marina said in English, screwing up her eyes and sliding out of his arms.

As they strolled back under the darkening skies of the Catskills, Marina told Simon that she used to work at Bluebell Inn, but this summer her parents wanted her to rest before college.

"I'm bored out of my mind. Imagine, it's either my family or the other Russian kids. There's nothing to do here."

"Do you have older siblings?" Simon asked.

"My brother Tolik. He and I are very close," Marina said, voice growing serious.

"What's his story?" Simon asked.

"He studies design at FIT. Very talented, very chic. My dad's barely speaking to him. He doesn't get such things."

Simon didn't ask more questions.

At breakfast the following morning Madame Yankelson, red roses climbing the twin trellises of her chiffon top, came up to their table, said a perfunctory hello to the grandmothers, and turned her gaze onto Simon.

"Young man, I would like it very much if you could spend some time with me," she said like an ageless actress in a radio play. "Please finish your breakfast, and my friend Lydia and I will look forward to seeing you at our usual post near the column by the main entrance."

A Moscow tomcat Simon may have been, but he was also a polite Jewish boy, and he couldn't very well say "No" or "I'm busy." Half an hour later, he stood in front of Madame Yankelson like a cadet at graduation exercises. She raised herself from her chair, threaded her soft arm through his, and he thought of hotdogs and buns, of Rabelais's oversized lovers, and also of Marina who would see him walking the same path but in Madame Yankelson's company.

"Take me to the lake, darling," Madame Yankelson said and led Simon across the meadow. "I'm leaving the parasol with you," she said to Lydia Shmukler, who silently nodded. From her white rocking chair, Madame Yankelson picked up a sequined purse the shape of a Maltese dog.

As they walked across the front lawn in the direction of the lake, Madame Yankelson put more weight on his right arm, as though trying to shift the direction.

"I know a secluded spot. There's a little bench there, and a marvelous view of the mountains," she said to Simon.

Instead of following the main alley, they veered off to the left, walking on a narrower path, which first dropped, then corrected its course. They finally came to a clearing with the promised bench and ensnared shrubs behind its back. Through an opening between tree trunks, one could see three bands of color—milky-blue sky, pea-green woods, and ink-grey road. Like a child's innocent painting, uncluttered by people.

"I would like you to read some of your poems to me," said Madame Yankelson, half turning to Simon and resting her bare arm on the back of the bench.

"My poems?" Simon muttered. "How do you know I write poems?"

"I read, my young friend, I read émigré magazines," she replied.

"Well, perhaps another time, Madame Yankelson," he said, somehow unable to put things right.

"I will be your best audience," Madame Yankelson insisted.

She took a thin brown cigarette out of her purse.

"I don't suppose you smoke, no? Well, you should know that I've been inspiring poets since I was a young lady." Holding the cigarette between her thumb and index finger, Madame Yankelson inhaled with affect. "You don't believe me?" she uttered with a labored laugh.

"No, I—"

"Mayakovsky himself was very fond of me, you know."

"Mayakovsky?"—now Simon couldn't hide his curiosity. It wasn't very often that one ran into people who knew the great poet.

"To explain I would have to tell you my age. And a true lady never reveals her age," said Madame Yankelson, making the kind of upward motion of her neck and cheekbones that was meant to pull back the furrows and wrinkles.

"Madame Yankelson, you're as young as you look," Simon said, horrified by the platitudes he was prepared to spout.

"Thank you, you're becoming a very dear friend," she said, removing a perfumed handkerchief from her purse. She waved the handkerchief, letting its skein brush against her lips.

"We moved from Riga to Moscow in 1925. I was thirteen," Madame Yankelson said, beginning her story. "My father was a renowned gemologist. He started working as an expert at the Central Jewelry Trust."

"So you're originally from Riga," Simon interrupted.

"You're a student of literature. You must have heard of my famous relative, Roman?" said Madame Yankelson.

"Roman Yankelson is your relative? The great medievalist?"

"My second cousin. Same last name. Their branch is also from Riga," Madame Yankelson affirmed, her voice feigning indifference. "Roman and I were a few years apart. When we emigrated, he was living in Boston, actually in Cambridge. I believe he had already retired. My late husband, too, was still alive, and we saw Roman in Manhattan when he was in town for a conference. I can't say he was dying to embrace his long-lost relatives."

"Why not?" Simon asked, naively.

"He had himself baptized, you know. Non-Jewish wife, non-Jewish family. You know how it goes. . . . " A toadish frown crept onto Madame Yankelson's face, but she immediately chased it away with her white fleshy hand.

"I said to him: 'Romochka, why do you need this nonsense? You want to write about Prince Igor, be my guest, but you don't need to go to their church and convert to feel more Slavic.' I don't think Roman or his Slovak wife liked hearing this. And he didn't even ask about the family that stayed behind in Riga. Still, Roma was my cousin, and when he passed on, I went down to Boston for his funeral."

"Madame Yankelson," Simon asked, trying to steer the conversation back to Mayakovsky and poetry. "You moved to Moscow from Riga—"

"Oh yes, in 1925." She picked up the dangling story. "Moscow was terribly overcrowded. At first we lived in an awful hole in the wall—even though my father was getting a very good salary and had connections. Finally—this was already 1926—my father managed to secure two rooms in a very decent apartment. Communal, of course, but that's the way it was back in those days. We moved to Gendrikov Lane, a very nice central location—you're from Moscow, you should know where it is."

"Vaguely," Simon said. "Isn't it somewhere near the Taganka Theater?"

Madame Yankelson sighed and dabbed off tiny beads of dew on her forehead.

"I was a girl, but already a young woman," she continued. "Now imagine: we're moving in. It's a hot sunny day in June. My father is at his office, my mother is running around and supervising the movers, and I'm just standing in everybody's way, wearing a lovely little sailor dress with ribbons and frills, taking everything in. And suddenly I see a big handsome man with a shaved head descending the stairs. At first I thought he was mean-spirited, but then he smiled at me—not even a full smile, but a half smile and a flicker in his eyes—and I could tell he was a gentle soul. 'Hello, young lady,' he said. 'Let's get acquainted. I'm Mayakovsky.' 'I'm Violetta Yankelson,' I said. 'Are you by chance related to my good friend Romka Yankelson?' he asked me in such a way that I felt I could trust him completely. And, may the Lord punish me if I'm lying to you, I felt that I would have done anything for this beautiful sad man. Anything."

"So you lived in the same building as Mayakovsky?" Simon asked, just to make sure he understood her correctly. The whole story was so fabulous.

"Yes, after 1926. And still after he shot himself. That was in 1930, I remember the day I found out like it was yesterday. They lived one floor above us. Mayakovsky and the Briks. Lilya was legally Brik's wife, and Mayakovsky loved her madly. She ruined his life, you know that, don't you?"

"What was he like?" Simon asked.

"Mayakovsky? A genius. And such a gallant man. He was always so kind to us. My parents worshipped him."

Madame Yankelson wiped the corners of her eyes with a thumb wrapped in the handkerchief. They sat for about a minute without speaking. All around them on the clearing, grasshoppers stammered away, dragonflies juddered in midflight, bees pulverized the mountain air. The life of insects went about its hourly tasks, replete with small sounds and vibrations, and yet indifferent to the fluctuations of the human spirit.

"Madame Yankelson, should we head back?"

"Back?" she repeated, momentarily confused, but then, regaining clarity of mind, she lifted her body from the bench. Clutching her white purse with one hand, she leaned on Simon's elbow with the other. They walked on the path and, quite innocently and thoughtlessly, just trying to find his way out of the encroaching silence, he said to Madame Yankelson:

"I'm ashamed to admit but I've never been to Riga. We used to go to Pärnu every summer."

Suddenly, as if picking up a forgotten thread in the labyrinth of her past, she stopped, looked at Simon with stern passion, and cried out:

"I love Riga and I hate it. It's the place of my birth; it's a city of death. My parents had the foolishness to go to Riga in 1940 to visit my grandparents. My older brother was a young air force pilot stationed in the north. I was a recent university graduate. We didn't stop them, and we were never to see them again. Killed at Rumbula . . ."

Madame Yankelson and Simon parted in front of the main entrance, and he could see that her companion, Lydia Shmukler, a silent sentinel, was waiting in her chair. Simon waved to her, said a formal goodbye to Madame Yankelson, and ran up four flights of stairs to his garret. He collapsed and slept until lunch.

The Sunday night dance was one of the high points of the vacationers' week at Bluebell Inn. Simon was already a little anxious that Madame Yankelson would again decide to unburden herself and nominate him as her dance partner, but, luckily for him, she complained of a migraine and said she wasn't going to be at the "evening ball." Simon was standing on the front porch, flanked by both grandmothers. For some inexplicable reason, Styopa's grandmother, who was usually pretty tight-lipped when it came to other people's lives, looked crookedly at Madame Yankelson and hissed,

"You're a vile woman, Violetta."

"You should go back to the mountains," Madame Yankelson said without malice.

"I am in the mountains," Styopa's grandmother threw back.

"I mean the Caucasus, where you're from. In civilized society, people are broad-minded. And you think it's the Middle Ages and that they still practice honor killings." Madame Yankelson had the last word.

From where Simon was standing, he could see Marina playing rainbow ball with her little sister at the far end of the front lawn. The two sisters, both wearing skorts that were in fashion that summer, and both clad in green tops, formed a wondrous praying mantis in the freshly mowed grass.

The main dining room had been converted into the dance floor. Basya from Minsk tended the bar. There was a dj and a silver disco ball multiplying the magenta and indigo lights. Marina's grandfather and father sported identical, groomed barrel mustaches of the sort that they used to call a "Cossack mustache" in the old country. Marina's father was dressed in a light seersucker suit; a shiny cummerbund kept his gut in place. The grandfather, a retired artillery officer, clicked his heels, bowed slightly with his head only, and asked Simon's grandmother to dance. He brought her back, flushed up and smiling, and asked Styopa's grandmother for the next dance, which happened to be "Lady in Red." Simon stood there in a group with Marina, her parents and sister, wanting to steal Marina from her family.

"So you're from Moscow. The capital," Marina's father barked into Simon's ear.

"Uh huh."

"Who are you studying to be?" the father asked, phrasing the question precisely the way most of their compatriots did—not *what* are you studying or majoring in but who, *who* you're studying to be.

"I'm studying literature," Simon answered, irritated by the question's bare-knuckled truth.

"Literature?" Marina's father repeated, as though the word tasted rancid on his tongue.

"Yes, literature, and I also write," Simon said, thinking of his short story, which had just come out in a New York émigré magazine. And of the Russian writer with meaty jowls and terribly sad eyes, whom Simon might have seen on the road to Roscoe . . .

"Well, young people," the older of the Brooklyn Cossacks said to Simon and Mira, "why are you standing? Dance and enjoy."

Simon led Marina to the floor, feeling her father's stare on his back and shoulders.

In places like Bluebell Inn one quickly surrenders to routine. For Simon this meant cheese blintzes for breakfast; tennis on the balding courts; boating and fishing for crappies and perch; afternoon naps in his overheated garret. And also much less English and much more Russian than he had gotten used to during his first American year.

When Madame Yankelson and Simon passed each other, she would say a theatrical "Hello, my dear friend." He would be walking across the front lawn and see her, sitting on her white throne, fleshy hands clasped on her bosom. Her gaze was long, reproachful. Simon's grandmother didn't say anything, but Styopa's grandmother never spared a venomous comment. Something was eating her, something she wanted to keep to herself but couldn't. And only Petya the pool attendant openly teased Simon about Madame Yankelson.

"How's the love affair going?" he said through the teeth, jerking his head in the direction where Madame Yankelson held court.

"Which one?" Simon retorted.

"Did you know we call her 'Granny Love?'"

"Very funny. And I call her 'Pique Dame.'"

"What's that?"

"It's a Pushkin story and an opera."

"I see." Petya spat out a stem of ryegrass he held between his teeth.

"You and Marina make a handsome couple," he said to Simon after breakfast on his last full day at Bluebell Inn. "Don't make a mess of it."

"Worry about your own life, pal," Simon replied in Russian, and Petya just shrugged his shoulders and ambled off in the direction of the pool.

Their strolls under the watchful eyes of the Russian immigrants. The meadows, cornices, and porches where Marina and Simon stood kissing at dusk, making wistful promises. They had talked about visiting each other once a month, his driving up to Binghamton, her taking a bus to Providence. It sounded, vaguely, sweetly, like an American movie Simon had yet to live. Prior to emigration, he had only dated girls who lived in or studied in Moscow. The whole institution of long-distance dating was practically nonexistent in his Soviet youth, unless it was framed by the scenario of a boy drafted to the military and a girl waiting or pretending to wait. And there were also the differences between Marina's background and Simon's, which the English language of love masked but never obliterated.

Marina shared a room with her second cousin Regina, whose name suggested different nicknames to the Russian and the English ear.

"Can you sneak out tonight?" Simon had asked Marina on the eve of his departure.

"My room's next to my parents.'"

"Won't your mom be sleeping?"

"Yes. But Regina reads late at night. She will babble."

"So let her babble."

"The whole place will soon know."

"Don't they know already?" he asked.

"What they know is not that," Marina said, and he had to take for face value the promise trapped inside her words.

Their last full day at Bluebell Inn was a Saturday, and Simon and the grandmothers were expecting guests. Styopa was coming with his former BU classmate Borya Glikman, whose parents and Simon's parents had also known each other in Moscow. Styopa and Borya were supposed to drive up early on Saturday, spend the day with them, stay the night at the hotel, and then head down to New York City for a reunion with another Russian college friend. But they didn't arrive until after supper.

Simon had never cared for Borya Glikman back in Moscow. He was snotty and conceited. As an eight- and nine-year-old he detested hockey and soccer, and showed off his knowledge of poetry, something kids in Simon's school would have found unforgiveable. But for some reason Styopa admired Borya. He called him "Bor," as in Niels Bohr. Ten years had gone by, and now Bor's Americanized self greeted Simon on the main porch of Bluebell Inn. He had black oversized spectacles, Elvis sideburns and a plush gut. In one hand he held a duffel bag, in the other a smoldering cigarette, which almost burned Simon's cheek as Bor motioned to hug him.

Styopa and Bor quickly completed the expected round of hellos and pleasantries. They left the two grandmothers on the porch, and a few minutes later Bor was already mixing Southern Comfort with cranberry juice and cutting up apples and cheddar cheese they had picked up at the general store up the road.

"What's Southern Comfort?" Simon asked.

"Where're you from?" Bor answered with a question.

"Moscow, actually, same place as you."

"He's only been here a year," Styopa said, rubbing his hands.

"Southern Comfort and cranberry juice is the best summer drink," Bor instructed Simon. "Try this," he handed him a white plastic cup. "Isn't it good?"

"Smells like cheap cognac," Simon said.

Styopa kept looking out the window onto the front lawn and yelling out, "Oy, this feels so good, so good." Bor was rhythmically chewing slabs of apple with cheese and replenishing their drinks.

"So how's Rhode Island?" Bor asked Simon, grinning.

"Brown's great," Simon replied in Russian. "But the town is a bore," he added, both to show off his English and to rile up Styopa's friend.

"I'm getting a modeling agency off the ground," Bor said, laziness in his voice. "I should probably come down to Providence and set up some interviews. I'll need some help. Are you game?"

"I don't know," Simon answered.

"You don't know?" Bor repeated the words. He was quickly becoming drunk, and his drunkenness brought out aggression.

"So how's love life, boys?" Bor asked, his pumpkinseed eyes drawing a curved line on the wall of his garret.

"It's wonderful, just wonderful," Styopa bleated. "You are my best friends in the whole wide world."

"He's still a cherry, you know," Bor said, pointing at Styopa with the bottle of Southern Comfort. "A nice little Jewish cherry."

Styopa rolled his eyes, his head bobbing like a balloon in the air.

"Cut the crap, Bor, he's not a cherry," Simon said.

"What, you let him fuck you?" Bor said.

"Leave Styopa alone," Simon grabbed Bor by the collar of his palm tree shirt and twisted it, pressing him to the garret's nearest low corner.

"I'm not a cherry," Styopa said in a voice that teetered between idiotic laughter and whining. "No-no-no."

"He has a girlfriend," Simon said to Bor, and he felt like he was back in summer camp outside Moscow, and a bully was taunting a bashful ten-year-old Styopa, and a nine-year-old Simon was punching the bully on his fat red lip.

"Easy, friend, I was joking," Bor wheezed, trying to peel Simon's hand off his throat. "This isn't Russia, you know. No need to get physical."

They all sat for a few minutes without speaking. Then Bor poured more Southern Comfort, neat this time. Bor and Styopa soon left, both of them unsteady on their feet, and Simon had trouble falling asleep in the hot garret. A mad orchestra of chirping and flickering noises wafted into his room, but he didn't want to shut the window because the humid air was suffocating. He felt tired after the liquor and the near fight. He was thinking about Marina and when they would see each other again. And then thoughts about Bor's outburst of aggression and doubts about a career in literature snowballed. . . . He must have finally drifted off because he did not remember the old ungreased hinges squeaking and the door opening . . .

She stood at the threshold of his world like an old undine brought back from retirement. Roused by the air current, her translucent white gown was beating, like a sail, at the heavy mast of her body. An unyielding thirst for life moistened her cinnamon lips. Desire burned in her eyes, and this light nearly paralyzed Simon in his bed. He labored to lift himself up on his elbows.

"Madame Yankelson, what are you doing here?"

"Not another word." She stepped closer, pressing her right index finger to her lips.

Struggling to find the right expression, the kind of language that would tactfully ward off the old lady who may have been sundowning, Simon finally uttered,

"Madame Yankelson, you cannot be here."

She stood so close to his bed that in the light of the moon coming in through the slanted roof he could see the palimpsest of her makeup, smell the wilted lily-of-the-valley scent of her body.

"I beg you, don't send me away," Madame Yankelson pleaded with her voice and long arms.

"Madame Yankelson, please. I have nothing but respect for—"

"Just let me have one kiss. To seal our hallowed friendship. And I will be your muse for eternity," she said desperately.

And it was then that Marina Ayzenbaum appeared. She froze in the doorway. On Marina's face Simon read horror—horror and incomprehension. Hands pressed to her face, she dashed out of the room.

"Get out, you old bat. Now see what you've done." Simon threw these words at Madame Yankelson and ran out after Marina, but it was too late.

In the morning, after breakfast, Marina's mother accosted Simon in the hotel lobby.

"Marinochka told me everything," she said, revulsion in her voice. "You are a pervert. My husband would have ripped your throat out. Be grateful he isn't here."

She turned and walked away, carrying a bagel in one hand and a banana in the other. The bagel and banana were probably for Marina, whom Simon never saw again.

For the first hour of their drive back to Boston the grandmothers bickered over Marina's grandfather.

"You acted like some young tart," Styopa's grandmother berated Simon's grandmother. "Flirting at your age is indecent."

"And you're jealous," Simon's grandmother replied.

"Me jealous?" Styopa's grandmother pushed on. "What's to be jealous about? Some old mushroom with ribbons on his chest?"

"Please stop, you two," Simon yelled, turning to the back seat. "You'll probably never see Marina's grandfather again. He lives in Canarsie Beach."

"Where's that?" Simon's grandmother asked, disappointment in her voice.

"You don't even know, that's where," Styopa's grandmother said, her voice more conciliatory. "It's in Brooklyn."

"So what, I could visit him there," Simon's grandmother replied. "Walk on the beach. Hear Russian performers."

From Tap-on-Thee Bridge all the way to New Haven the grandmothers pouted, studying the American landscape. By the time they reached Boston they had made up and were talking about their old neighborhood in Moscow—between Belorussky train station and Dynamo soccer stadium. The dear old haunts where the grandmothers used to stroll with Simon and Styopa in prams.

Almost thirty years had passed since the first American summer of Simon Reznikov. Simon had now lived in America for ten years longer than he had in Russia, and yet his Soviet childhood and youth still had a grip on his memory.

Simon was still based in Brookline, a near suburb of Boston that was urban enough for his Moscow breeding. His biography of Felix Gregor, the Jewish writer from Prague, had come out in 1996. Tenured and promoted, Simon had moved from the cozy women's college west of Boston to a much larger campus on the Charles. Simon now mostly wrote nonfiction, usually for a New York-based magazine with a Jewish slant, and occasionally he contributed a short story to one of the better-known literary quarterlies.

He married on the late side, his professional life already in order. His wife, Kate, who was born in Chicago to parents originally from St. Petersburg, ran an international college-placement firm, and many of her clients were wealthy Russians, Ukrainians and Kazakhs. Simon and Kate had two sons and a daughter, each less than two years apart. At home they spoke a mixture of Russian and English.

Simon's marriage and family life might be, as an immigrant Dostoevsky would have put it, the subject of a *new story*, but the present one ends with a return to Simon's American beginnings.

Time relentlessly took as it generously gave. Just days after Simon's older son had turned seven, his ninety-six-year-old grandmother died in her sleep. Simon's parents retired and bought an apartment in Hollywood, Florida, where they now spent the colder months of the year.

Simon and his family were living only a few miles from the suburb where Styopa Agarun had settled with his Odessa-born wife and two sons. They saw each other once, maybe twice a year. It had evolved into a virtual friendship. They followed each other's lives through Facebook, and thus Simon learned that Styopa had sold his software company, bought a summer place in New Seabury, driven his older son to Atlanta, where he was starting college. They had always been different, Simon and Styopa, and in one's late forties differences stood more and more in the way of old friendships. And yet, every time Simon and Styopa talked on the phone or ran into each other, they trusted each other and let their hearts speak.

In the winter of 2015, Simon heard from his parents that Styopa was getting a divorce. He picked up the phone and called. Styopa spoke in a subdued, creaky voice.

"Wait until you see me," Styopa said. "I've lost thirty pounds with this divorce thing."

"Skinny Styopa," Simon said, thinking back to the time they arrived in America and he saw Styopa after many years of not seeing him, belly bouncing under a yellow polo shirt.

"That's right. Had to buy all new clothes. One should get divorced more often."

"Do you ever speak to Borya Glikman?" Simon asked, sensing that Styopa didn't want to talk about his family life.

"I actually just had an email from him. Bor's doing fine. He lives on Staten Island. Runs a philanthropic organization. Not quite sure what they do."

"Is he married?" Simon asked.

"Yep, to a really pretty girl. Petite, with big eyes. Works as a public defender. Parents from Ukraine, someplace wild. I think he met her at Bluebell Inn that time we drove down to see you. Remember?"

"I feel like it happened in some other life," Simon said.

"You still had that newcomer look," Styopa said, and they soon hung up, both thinking it would be a while before they would speak again.

It was different this time. That same evening, a collection of photographs arrived in Simon's email. He scrolled through the pictures, recognizing and not recognizing the place. Grass stood waist high on the lawn in front of the resort's main building. "FOR SALE" signs were nailed to a billboard. The buildings hadn't been painted in years, and the white gutters were stained with inky spots like an old bookkeeper's arthritic fingers. A crimson curtain, like a salamander's fluttering tongue, peered through a broken window in one of the garrets. Paths and alleys had virtually disappeared from the grounds, and the lake's water was invisible under bottle-green muck. It turned out that a New York photographer with a Polish last name, who had grown up in the 1960s going to Bluebell Inn with his family, took a series of pictures while on a visit to the Catskills, and Styopa sent Simon a link to the photographer's website.

Simon called Styopa back after his wife and kids had gone to bed.

"These photos . . . I was shocked. Do you know what happened?"

"After we spoke I did some checking," said Styopa. "Turns out the resort has been closed for years. Apparently they tried to sell it to a luxury spa developer, but the deal fell through. It's not even an active listing. So sad. You know, I was there every summer between 1980 and 1986."

"I was only there for less than two weeks. And I still felt sadness looking at these photos," Simon could hear Styopa breathing into the phone, and Styopa could probably hear him typing on his laptop.

"Remember Madame Yankelson?" Styopa asked, after a pause.

"Don't I? She was something else."

"She was a character. I got to know her very well over the six summers. . . . She was my—"

"I know, Styopa," Simon said, suddenly feeling like he was about to choke on tears. "You don't need to explain."

They hung up, this time forgoing the usual promise of getting together. Simon walked across the living room to the picture window overlooking Beacon Street and the T tracks. Upstairs, in their bedrooms, his Boston-born kids were sleeping. Tropical fish slept in their illuminated tanks, slept without sleeping, like restive time itself. Leaning against the black upright piano, the pages from his older son's songbook were opened to "The Merry Farmer." Simon studied their neighborhood's evening landscape, blocks of blackened snow standing four feet tall after what had been a month of weekly Nor'easters. The downcast streetlights added a warm sepia glow to the snowbanks. Simon pressed his forehead against the cold glass, closing his eyes. Then he went back to his office and touched the trackpad, waking up his laptop. He felt the current of memory flowing through him, bridging his first American summer and the new life he had fashioned after three decades in America.

In one of the pictures Simon saw himself standing with Marina Ayzenbaum at the edge of the meadow in front of Bluebell Inn. They were holding hands. Marina squinted in the sun, her freckles violently orange, the latticed strap of her bra sliding off her shoulder.

Then they both heard a window slamming with the fervor of the whole century. They looked up at the hotel and saw a cloth flying from a second-floor room. Of course it was Madame Yankelson's shawl, dainty like a Russian poet's promise of love. Long, like the shadow of Jewish exile. White, like an immigrant's flag of surrender.

1999–2018
Boston—Brookline—South Chatham, Mass.

Acknowledgments

An earlier version of the final section of "Brotherly Love" appeared as "Sonetchka" in Maxim D. Shrayer, *Yom Kippur in Amsterdam* (Syracuse: Syracuse University Press/Library of Modern Jewish Fiction, 2009). Copyright © 2009 by Maxim D. Shrayer.

The author gratefully acknowledges the support of Boston College.

I would like to thank Christopher Soldt of Boston College Graphic Services for his assistance with the cover illustration.

I am grateful to Stuart Allen, Alessandra Anzani, Matthew Charlton, Jenna Colozza, Kira Nemirovsky and their colleagues at Cherry Orchard Books—Academic Studies Press for welcoming this Russian immigrant to their book haven.

Sharon Hart-Green, Karen von Kunes, Boris Lanin, Holli Levitsky, Pavel Lembersky, David Shrayer-Petrov, Veronika Tuckerova, and Olga Zilberbourg read and commented on the manuscript. I owe them all a debt of gratitude.

Without the love and support of my family—my wife Karen, our daughters Mira and Tatiana, and my parents Emilia and David— I would still be trying to write a book titled *A Russian Immigrant*.

About the Author

The bilingual author and scholar Maxim D. Shrayer (Максим Д. Шраер) was born in Moscow in 1967 to a Jewish-Russian family, and spent over eight years as a refusenik. He and his parents, the writer and doctor David Shrayer-Petrov and the translator Emilia Shrayer, left the USSR and immigrated to the United States in 1987, after spending a summer in Austria and Italy. Shrayer attended Moscow University, Brown University, and Rutgers University, and received a PhD at Yale University in 1995. He is Professor of Russian, English, and Jewish Studies at Boston College, where he cofounded the Jewish Studies Program, and is an associate at Harvard University's Davis Center, where he founded the Project on Russian and Eurasian Jews. Shrayer edits the book series *Jews of Russia & Eastern Europe and Their Legacy* at Academic Studies Press.

Shrayer has authored and edited over fifteen books of criticism, biography, nonfiction, fiction, poetry, and translation. He is the author of the acclaimed literary memoirs *Waiting for America: A Story of Emigration* and *Leaving Russia: A Jewish Story* (finalist of the 2013 National Jewish Book Awards), the story collection *Yom Kippur in Amsterdam*, and three collections of Russian-language poetry. He has also edited and cotranslated from the Russian four books of fiction by his father, David Shrayer-Petrov, most recently the novel *Doctor Levitin*.

In 2007, Shrayer won a National Jewish Book Award for his two-volume *Anthology of Jewish-Russian Literature*. His book *I Saw It: Ilya Selvinsky and the Legacy of Bearing Witness to the Shoah* appeared in 2013. Shrayer's *Bunin and Nabokov: A History of Rivalry*, was published in 2014 in Moscow and became a national bestseller. His recent works include *Zalman's Disappearance*, a collection of Russian-language stories, *With or Without You: The Prospect for*

Jews in Today's Russia, and *Voices of Jewish-Russian Literature: An Anthology.* Shrayer's publications have been translated into nine languages.

Shrayer is the recipient of a number of awards and fellowships, including those from the Guggenheim Foundation, the National Endowment for the Humanities, the Rockefeller Foundation, and the Bogliasco Foundation. He lectures widely on topics ranging from the legacy of the refusenik movement and the experience of ex-Soviet Jews in America to Shoah literature and Jewish-Russian culture. Shrayer lives in Massachusetts with his wife, Dr. Karen E. Lasser, a medical researcher and physician, and their daughters Mira and Tatiana. They divide their time between Brookline and South Chatham, Massachusetts.

For more information, visit Shrayer's website at

www.shrayer.com.

Praise for *A Russian Immigrant*

"'All the new thinking is about loss. / In this way it resembles all the old thinking.' That's Robert Hass in his poem 'Meditation at Lagunitas,' but it's also the imperative behind Maxim D. Shrayer's beautiful and haunting troika of novellas that limn the shifting patterns of contemporary Russian-Jewish immigrant experience with tenderness and charm. Shrayer is an elegant, generous writer always ready to salvage what matters most from lives shipwrecked by history."

     —Jonathan Wilson, author of *Kick and Run: Memoir with Soccer Ball*

"Forget all the slapstick, Moscow-on-the-Hudson, burlesque treatments of Jewish Russian émigré life you've ever read. If you want the honest, beautifully rendered, and deeply compelling truth about what it's like to be a Russian immigrant in America, these three braided novellas by the very talented Maxim D. Shrayer are all you need."

     —Eileen Pollack, author of *The Bible of Dirty Jokes*

"Maxim D. Shrayer's meticulously crafted and richly nuanced tryptic of novellas reads like a wistful goodbye to the shifting geopolitical and economic landscape on both sides of the pond. *A Russian Immigrant* is a loving farewell to things past and disintegrated: from the protagonist's scholarly sojourn in Prague to his nostalgia-drenched memories of romance and brotherly love of his last Soviet vacation in Estonia to the show-stopping comedy pair of elderly ladies in the once popular Catskills resort now on the brink of losing its erstwhile splendor. The sensitive, intelligent and compassionate young

Simon Reznikov who never misses his chance to assert his Russian-American biculturalism—and his Jewishness—or follow his heart in pursuit of romantic love, is a joy to observe as he moves from adolescence to early adulthood. Shrayer's protagonist is bound to take pride of place among other renowned characters of coming-of-age fiction and beyond."

—Pavel Lembersky, author of *Here's Looking At You, Kid*

"The wry and poignant novellas in Maxim D. Shrayer's new collection, *A Russian Immigrant*, are a valuable addition to the literature of exile, displacement, and the Diaspora. Shrayer's protagonist, Simon Reznikov, is a scholar researching a 'writer without a biography.' The three novellas dig deep Reznikov's Russian Jewish soul as we witness his love affairs gone awry, wittily and tenderly portrayed in Shrayer's sparkling prose."

—Tony Eprile, author of *The Persistence of Memory*

CPSIA information can be obtained
at www.ICGtesting.com
Printed in the USA
FSHW022140090819
60888FS